Advance Praise for

THE WEIGHT OF EVERYTHING

"Prepare to be captivated by strong, resourceful, artistic Sarah as she holds her family together after tragedy. In the minutes she can steal from caretaking, adjusting to a new school, and navigating a could-be-beautiful relationship, Sarah works on an art project that reveals her connection to Guatemala's painful past. Written with clarity and insight, this book is driven by devotion to family, tender romance, and Sarah's determination to use her artistic talent to right a wrong. A must-read for anyone who loves to cheer for a brave young woman!"

—Rebecca Balcárcel, Pura Belpré Honor winning author of *The Other Half of Happy*

"A poignant, raw, and emotional story of grief, loss, and the courage it takes to fight for our beliefs—and ourselves."

—Crystal Maldonado, author of *Fat Chance, Charlie Vega* and *No Filter and Other Lies*

"*The Weight of Everything* is a beautifully told, breathtaking story about a young woman's fight to care for her wounded family while remaining true to the call of love and an awakening social conscience."

—Francisco Stork, author of *On the Hook*

THE WEIGHT OF EVERYTHING

EVERYTHING

MARCIA ARGUETA MICKELSON

🌿 carolrhoda LAB
MINNEAPOLIS

Carolrhoda Lab®
An imprint of Lerner Publishing Group, Inc.
241 First Avenue North
Minneapolis, MN 55401 USA

For reading levels and more information, look up this title at
www.lernerbooks.com.

Image Credits: Joanna Dorota/Shutterstock; Olga_C/Shutterstock; croco_d_ulya/
Shutterstock; Anastasiia Gevko/Shutterstock.

Main body text set in Janson Text LT Std.
Typeface provided by Adobe Systems.

Library of Congress Cataloging-in-Publication Data

Names: Mickelson, Marcia Argueta, author.
Title: The weight of everything / Marcia Argueta Mickelson.
Description: Minneapolis : Carolrhoda Lab, [2023] | Audience: Ages 12–18. |
    Audience: Grades 10–12. | Summary: Following her mother's tragic death,
    seventeen-year-old Sarah takes on the role of caretaker to her grieving father and
    younger brother, which leaves little time and emotional energy for a relationship,
    but when a school project helps her rediscover her love of art, her perspective shifts.
Identifiers: LCCN 2022023455 (print) | LCCN 2022023456 (ebook) |
    ISBN 9781728475356 | ISBN 9781728479187 (ebook)
Subjects: CYAC: Grief—Fiction. | Painting—Fiction. | Dating—Ficiton. |
    High schools—Fiction. | Schools—Fiction. | Hispanic Americans—Fiction.
Classification: LCC PZ7.M581924 We 2023 (print) | LCC PZ7.M581924 (ebook) |
    DDC [Fic] —dc23

LC record available at https://lccn.loc.gov/2022023455
LC ebook record available at https://lccn.loc.gov/2022023456

Manufactured in the United States of America
1-52097-50571-9/30/2022

PARA MI MAMÁ, POR TODA SU SABIDURÍA

CHAPTER ONE

When Vic called, I thought my dad had died. Vic's first phone call had been to tell me that my mom had died; my dad had been too distraught to make the call himself. Vic's second call caused me to pack up everything from my dorm room into my Toyota and drive back home.

Vic said my dad had had a nervous breakdown, though I don't think that's the term people use anymore. It's been almost three months since that call, but the heart-pounding feeling of disaster I experienced that day filters its way into my mind as I sit in first-period physics.

Mr. Lemmon takes attendance and starts talking about the syllabus and his expectations. I pull my cell phone out of my backpack and let out a small breath when I see there are no notifications. I keep my phone on my lap as Mr. Lemmon reviews the class weight of each type of assignment.

Today is the first day I've left my dad alone since I came back from boarding school, and this overwhelming thought keeps creeping into my mind, making it impossible to pay attention to Mr. Lemmon: *I shouldn't be here right now.*

I should be at home. School seems like such a triviality in light of what real life has to offer—a dead mom and a broken-down dad.

Mr. Lemmon is explaining the projects he expects us to complete when my phone buzzes. I think about Vic's phone call, but it isn't him. It's my retired neighbor, Wanda.

WANDA: Sarah, where are you? Are you home? Your father is outside howling. Can you hear him?

SARAH: No. I'm at school.

WANDA: Well, someone needs to make him stop. He's scaring all the dogs in the neighborhood. Buddy won't stop yelping.

SARAH: Okay, I'm coming home.

WANDA: Hurry. I don't want to have to call the police.

I should've stayed home today. I knew it. Being absent on the first day of your junior year in a brand-new school is less suspect than walking out in the middle of physics. I am currently walking out in the middle of physics. I hear Mr. Lemmon's voice trailing me down the hall.

"Sarah? Sarah!" he calls from the open door of his classroom.

But I don't turn around. I just keep up the half-walk/half-run that's going to get me to the main entrance. My phone vibrates, and I know it's Wanda again. I pick up my pace and run past the cold-colored lockers. I bolt through the front doors, leaving behind the frigid hallway and plunging right into the stifling Texas heat. The sun is searing, and I put up a hand to block it while I try to remember where, in this football-field-sized parking lot, I left my car.

I slow down, trying to catch my breath in the suffocating morning air as I approach the student parking. I answer the phone, which hasn't stopped buzzing. "Wanda?"

"I am outside trying to talk to him over the fence, but he won't stop howling. If you don't get over here, I'm calling the police."

I hear my dad in the background. He's crying in the same way he was when I first came home three months ago.

"Wait, Wanda. I'm coming. You know he won't do anything. Just wait." I spot my car and sprint over to it.

"You better hurry, Sarah. I'm sorry, but my nerves can't take it."

"I'm coming." I toss the phone onto the passenger seat and speed through the flashing lights of the school zone. I go over a speed bump too quickly and feel the effects as the bottom of my Toyota grinds against it. As I pull up into my driveway, Wanda is looking through the curtains of her front door.

I mouth *I'm sorry*, and Wanda shakes her head and pulls the curtains closed.

I hear him wailing in the backyard. I jog across our lawn and go around the side of the house.

He's lying on our old, weathered trampoline. His wails have turned into sobbing.

"Dad, what are you doing?" I climb onto the trampoline and sit in front of him.

"Sarah?" He opens his teary eyes and looks up at me.

"Wanda called me. She said you were crying so loudly that it was scaring her dog."

"I'm sorry. I'm sorry. I just came out here to clean the trampoline off so Steven could jump on it after school, but all I could think about was the day we bought it. She was so scared that Steven would fall off and get hurt, but I told her, Sarah will jump with him. Sarah will take care of him."

She refers to Mom. That's what he calls her now. It's as if the pronoun exists only to refer to Viviana Mosley.

"Remember, you used to jump with him? He would sit in the center and you would bounce him up and down."

"Yeah, I remember, Dad. Look, it's not good for you to be out here, okay? Wanda almost called the police."

"I'm sorry, Sarah. She's so unreasonable."

I suppress a frustrated sigh. "I had to leave school early for this."

"I'm sorry," he repeats. He pulls himself up, and we sit at the edge of the trampoline, our feet dangling over the side. "It's just so hard, Sarah. Everywhere I look, I'm reminded of what we lost." He wipes his face and turns to look at me. "You have her eyes." I've heard this a hundred different times from a hundred different people.

"Let's go inside," I say. I jump off the trampoline, and he follows me into the house. He goes straight upstairs to his room and throws himself into the recliner next to his unmade bed. I hover in the doorway.

"Dad, you can't keep going on like this."

No response.

I sit on the edge of his bed, grabbing the corner of the bedspread Mom bought two years ago in Amish country. "Should I ask Vic to come over?"

Vic is one of Dad's best friends, and one of the only people who stepped up for us when Mom died. He checks in regularly, drops off meals without making it feel like charity, and almost has Dad convinced to see a therapist. He and Dad worked together at UTSA, both of them history professors. He's the one who called me after Dad walked out of a class full of hundreds of students and Vic found him in his office, sobbing under his desk. His wife, Laura, was a big help right after Mom died, but I haven't seen her for a while. I know she keeps busy with their twelve-year-old twins.

"No, Sarah. Don't call Vic. I'm fine now."

Fine? I want to ask him what his definition of *fine* is. How can he say he's fine if he can't even make himself go back to work? We're basically living off dwindling savings, early withdrawal of retirement funds, and CDs that were meant to help pay my college tuition. At the rate I'm cashing out the CDs, there will be nothing left when I finally make it to college. We are definitely not fine. Dad's actions are out of my control, but they control me. I don't know how I'll even feel okay about going to school tomorrow.

A familiar bottle on his bedside table catches my eye. Some Scotch that my parents received from friends for Christmas years ago. It's been sitting on their small wine cabinet in the living room ever since. They'd always been mostly wine drinkers. Now the bottle is here in Dad's bedroom, half empty.

He turns on the television as the History Channel narrator introduces a documentary on ancient Chinese super ships.

I get up and close the door of his room.

After retrieving my backpack from my car, I pull off my ankle boots and drop onto the couch in the living room. My heart finally beats at its normal rate. I wipe my sweaty hands on my shorts, and I pull up my curly black hair with an elastic band I keep on my wrist. I considered cutting it before school started, but it's the same length as my mom's hair before she died. It's exactly how I want it right now. From my Mexican American mom, I inherited my rich skin tone and dark, curly hair. From my English American dad, I inherited my last name, Mosley, and that's about it.

With my fingertips, I dab at the back of my damp neck. I melt into the middle seat of our brown leather couch, facing Mom's bright red wingback chair. Next to it is the white basket of yarn and knitting needles that haven't been touched since before she died.

Today, it is six months and two days since she died. I gave Dad time to mourn, but it wasn't enough. No amount of time will ever be enough; I understand that. I don't feel any better about her death than I did six months ago, but I haven't stopped living. He doesn't want to live this life without her, though.

Nothing matters to him anymore. The children he helped create and nurture for years are only ghosts to him. Whatever affection he had for us seems to have died when she did. Maybe those feelings only existed because of her, and now that she's gone, we're gone to him too.

I stare at Mom's wingback chair, at the small square throw pillow that sits on the cushion. Mom would always put that pillow behind her lower back. It's kind of lost its shape from years of being tugged and pushed to make her more comfortable. On the front is a fading image of a red Gerber daisy with long petals and a pale yellow center.

I grab my backpack and take out a set of Sharpie markers I keep inside. I pull out a red Sharpie and take its cap off. I trace narrow petals on the top of my thigh and then color them in with a lighter shade of red. I draw one after the other in a circular shape, taking my time to color them in carefully.

Mom hated my Sharpie tattoos. After eight years of art lessons, Mom wanted me to do oil on canvas or watercolors, but this is my favorite medium. I like the idea of my art walking around rather than being stuck on a wall inside a room.

I color in the center, making it a bright yellow rather than the pale yellow showing on the aging throw pillow. After it's had enough time to dry, I dust it with baby powder from my small container, rubbing the powder in with my finger. I spray it with hairspray and rub some more. I look from the flower on Mom's throw pillow to the one on my thigh, taking in the details.

I close my eyes for a minute to rest them. I couldn't fall asleep last night—thinking about starting at a new school, wondering how Dad was doing, nervous about my brother's first day of third grade. Mom would've made Steven's first day amazing with her Texas toast for breakfast.

I jolt awake. I've been passed out on the couch all morning. I look at the clock and think of Steven. His bus will arrive in about three hours.

That gives me time to catch up on work. I go upstairs to my room and clear off some space on my desk. I pull out a pencil sketch I've been working on. I've been running an Etsy shop for about four months. My account has twenty-eight reviews, each with five stars. Customers send me photographs of their families, and I draw pencil portraits from the pictures. The more people in a portrait and the larger the size they choose, the more I'm able to charge. Currently, I'm drawing a portrait of a family of four—mom, dad, sister, brother—and they've requested a twelve-by-sixteen image. The money they paid for it is gone already, used for this week's groceries. I have two more orders waiting after this one.

I stare at the three-by-five photo I printed out. The mom has long blond hair, and I've been trying to perfect her bangs, but my pencil keeps stumbling over this one strand right above her left eye. Skipper wears a high bow, nearly covering part of her brother's hair, and has the most freckles I've ever tried to draw. The girl's name isn't really Skipper, but I've been calling her that since I started the portrait. She just looks like the mini version of her Barbie mother.

I finish most of Skipper, opting to procrastinate on the mass of dots splotched across her face. I set the portrait aside and decide to go meet Steven's bus.

I walk outside and sit on the curb. Across the street, Robert is weed-whacking Ms. Maldonado's path. I wave and receive a nod in return. Robert is retired and lives one street over. He makes his way up and down the streets trimming people's weeds wherever he finds unsatisfactory lawns.

I'm constantly amazed by the stamina and energy that comes from this more-than-seventy-year-old man. I heard Wanda say that he had bypass surgery a few years ago, but it doesn't slow him down. The only sign of his age is the thick patch of white hair on his head that matches the hair on his saggy chest—a chest I'm forced to look at way too often. He only wears a shirt when the temperature is below seventy.

I glance at our own lawn and wonder when he might make his way over here. Robert moves on to the next house, and the loud humming of his gas-powered weed-whacker begins again. Do we even have a weed-whacker in the garage? Probably, under all of Dad's gardening tools. He used to keep our yard beautifully manicured. Every year, he'd grow a huge garden in the back with tomatoes, peas, squash, peppers, zucchini, and a dozen different kinds of herbs.

Steven's bus comes into view at the corner, and I stand up and walk toward it. I wring my hands and pull on my fingers as I watch the kids descend from the bus one by one. My lanky brother steps off and watches his feet as he walks toward me.

"Hi, Steven. How was your first day?"

He looks at me and blinks. "Sarah? You said your school doesn't get out until four." He holds up his Astros key chain. "You said I had to let myself in and be sure to close the door behind me."

"I know. I just got out early today." I put my arm around him, and we walk together to the house.

At the front steps, Steven bends down to pick up the newspaper. Mom always insisted on keeping a newspaper subscription despite Dad and me telling her it's better online. Steven shares her fondness for an actual newspaper that can be held in one's hands. Lately I've thought about canceling the subscription since it's so expensive, but I can't bring myself to take it away from Steven.

Inside, he lets his backpack fall to the floor and takes the newspaper over to the table, discarding all the sections except for the sports. He scans the baseball scores. "The Phillies beat the Cubs, seven to two."

"That's a good score."

"The Mets won again. That's five games in a row. That's called a winning streak. Beat the Braves four to three."

I open a cupboard and scan its contents. "How about spaghetti for dinner?"

"Spaghetti sounds good. Can you melt some cheese on it?" Steven asks without taking his eyes off the newspaper. He continues running his finger along the box scores, his fingertips blackening with the action. "The Astros scored six runs in the top of the ninth. Six runs. The Astros pitcher had eight strikeouts."

"Do you like your new teacher?"

"Yeah, she's cool, but a little corny too. She thinks we're still little kids, tells us to put a bubble in our mouth when we walk down the hall. We're third graders now."

"But other than that, she's cool?"

Steven folds the newspaper in fourths. "Yeah. She let us pick our own seats, so that's cool in my book. I get to sit next to my friend Ryan. We just have to make sure we don't talk too much or she'll move us." He's still scanning the box scores, nodding and shaking his head at intervals. "The Astros pitcher almost pitched a perfect game last night. That would've been number twenty-four in MLB history, and the first time in Astros history." Steven loves numbers; everything makes more sense to him with numbers.

I retrieve a jar of off-brand tomato sauce from the pantry to go with the spaghetti and fill a pot with water. There should still be a half-full package of ground beef in the fridge that I can use for meatballs. They'd be better with some fresh garlic, but we don't have any.

"How's Dad?" Steven asks abruptly, as if he just remembered there's more going on in the world than just baseball.

"Okay, I guess. He had a rough day."

"I'm going to go say hi to him." Steven bounds up the stairs, and I follow.

"Hey, Dad," Steven says, entering the room. He goes over to Dad's recliner and gives him an awkward half-hug.

"Hey, Steven. How was school?"

"Good. The Astros won last night, beat the Twins. Did you see Javier almost pitched a perfect game?"

"No, I guess I missed that," Dad says, not taking his eyes off the TV.

"Mom says make your bed every day, Dad," Steven says, noticing the quilt thrown messily on the bed. "It's supposed to be the first thing we do in the morning when we wake up. She would want us to make our beds."

Dad stares at him for a minute before turning back to the TV.

"Bye, Dad," Steven says as he leaves he room. "I have to go type up the baseball scores." He keeps a spreadsheet with the box scores from all the baseball games, just to study it.

Back downstairs, I boil spaghetti and make meatballs as Steven consumes the newspaper. After I set the table, I take a tray into Dad's room. The History Channel is replaying a documentary on the Japanese internment. Dad is dozing in the recliner, the half-empty bottle of Scotch perched precariously between his legs. I pull it out of his weak grasp, screw the lid on, and put it on his dresser. The movement startles him awake, and he sits up with a gasp.

I bring a small folding table over to his recliner and set the tray down on it, handing him extra napkins.

"This looks really good," he says, taking a voracious bite.

I nod and walk toward the door. "You need something in your stomach besides booze."

"Sarah," he says, and I turn around. "Thank you."

I nod again and rush out. I hate taking care of him. Steven is different—he's my little brother, a boy with one parent dead and the other one nearly there. I take care of Steven happily, but a teenager shouldn't have to care for a parent. He's still supposed to be taking care of *us*.

CHAPTER TWO

In the morning, I check on Dad and find him asleep under a bundle of blankets like it isn't still ninety degrees out. The Amish quilt is on the floor at the foot of the bed, the purple and red squares brightening the dull room.

I walk Steven to his bus stop. When I try to grab his hand as we cross the street, he pushes it away.

"Sarah, I'm in third grade now. You can't hold my hand."

"Sorry," I say. "I forget." I withdraw my hand and adjust my pony tail instead. My hair is still damp from my shower but soft from the handful of curl cream I added.

As we approach the bus stop, I see a gathering of other kids. The younger ones have parents with them, but most kids Steven's age are huddled in groups together, with no parents.

"One move like that, and kids will make fun of me for the rest of the year." Steven carries his backpack over one shoulder. "But I *am* glad you're back home, Sarah. Now you can take me to Richards games on Fridays. I don't think Dad will go. He never wants to do anything anymore."

"He's going to get better, Steven."

He turns his brown eyes to me and forces a smile. "Have a good day. Give Richards a chance. I bet you'll like it."

I gave Richards High School a chance yesterday, and I

didn't like it, but I don't tell Steven that. I smile and give him a small wave as he walks toward the group of kids waiting for the bus.

He's right; I shouldn't be comparing Richards High School to the Austin Performing and Fine Arts Academy, the boarding school where I lived for freshman and most of sophomore years. Austin is a mere eighty miles from San Antonio, but my little academy is a world away from Richards, home of the Bears and over three thousand students.

After Mom's funeral, I went back to Austin PFA, thinking we all had to get on with our lives. But after Dad's breakdown, I came home. When Dad stopped working and isolated himself in his room, I knew I had no choice but to stay. A history professor who doesn't show up to class ultimately loses his job. And no salary equals no money for tuition at the Austin Performing and Fine Arts Academy.

I pass Ms. Maldonado's house, and the scent of her lilac bushes follows me as I cross the street. My eyes dart to the brick window box outside our dining room. I close my eyes, and for an instant I can imagine the yellow and white daffodils Mom planted each winter. They would bloom in spring and brighten the entire face of our house. Now, the window box is littered with leaves from our oak tree.

I have about forty minutes before I have to leave for school. Breakfast for Dad? No. He's still asleep.

I grab the pile of mail that's been collecting on the skinny oak table in the entryway. There's a utility bill and a phone bill. Those have become my responsibility.

Dad kept up with the bills at first. After he quit his job, I knew he'd started putting most of our expenses on his credit cards and pilfering from his savings to pay off the cards' monthly minimums. Toward the end of summer, though, I received a phone call saying that our power would be shut off if we didn't pay. That was when I realized he hadn't paid any bills in over three months.

I took charge of the bills, though not soon enough to keep his car from being repossessed. Now I pay the household expenses out of my disappearing college fund. I'm just grateful my car and the house are paid off.

Another envelope, addressed to Dad, catches my attention. It looks like a statement from his mutual fund company. I found out a month ago that he'd been cashing out his retirement funds, though I'm not sure what he's using that money for.

Scratch that. I'm fairly certain he's spending it on alcohol. I think he's only started on that Scotch because he's gotten sick of all the wine he's been consuming.

I want to open this letter to see how much money is still in his account. Is he using up all his retirement savings? Surely he knows the penalties and taxes associated with early withdrawal. I wonder if there will be any money left once he actually reaches retirement age.

But there's no time to think about that right now. I have to pay the bills online and make as much progress on my Etsy project as I can before school.

Student parking at Richards High School feels like half a mile from the actual building. I walk in and try to orient myself, but I think I came in a different entrance yesterday. I look around for a familiar face—after all, I went to middle school with some of these kids before I went to Austin PFA as a freshman—but I don't recognize anyone. I think I see the cafeteria up ahead and remember my class was just upstairs from there.

"Are you Sarah?" a guy about my age asks. He stops me near the cafeteria, at the base of the steps. He's about five inches taller than me, with dark bangs framing the deepest brown eyes I've ever seen.

"Yeah. How do you know my name?"

He smiles, crinkling his eyes. "I'm David Garza. I'm in your physics class, and Mr. Lemmon said your name like fifteen times yesterday when you left."

I cover my face, thinking ahead to physics when I'll have to face Mr. Lemmon. "Oh, jeez. Was he really mad?"

"Not mad. Just puzzled, I guess. He got over it once he realized you weren't coming back. Was everything okay?"

"Yeah, I just had a family emergency, and I had to leave school."

His amazing dark eyes widen, then squint as if he's trying to figure something out. "Wow, I'm sorry. I hope it wasn't too serious."

"Yeah, it's fine."

"Well, Lemmon's tough. He said we have a quiz every day over the previous day's notes." David takes a step away from the staircase, and I do the same. Streams of students are rounding the corner toward the stairs, and we're right in their path. "I took notes." David opens his backpack and pulls out a spiral notebook. "Want to take a picture of them, so you can look them over before class?"

"That would be great. Thank you." I pull out my phone and take pictures of two pages of handwritten notes. His handwriting is miniscule and light, and I hope I'll be able to decipher it later. "Thanks, really."

"No problem. See you in class." David turns to walk away and gives me a smile over his shoulder.

I smile back.

A blond guy about David's height taps him on the shoulder and starts up the stairs with him. He turns to look at me, and a smirk stretches his mouth as recognition sets in. He remembers me.

Finding my way around Richards is a challenge. This place is so different from PFA. Between periods, I take a picture of the ridiculously crowded hallway and send it to Alexa, my old roommate. She texts back right away with an open-mouthed emoji.

At least I manage to get to all my classes on time. I can tell that advanced art is going to be my favorite—and that Spanish might break me. I'm already questioning the logic of starting a new language my junior year. It's not like I need the foreign language credit. I started taking French classes in sixth grade—a full five years' worth of learning to parler tres bien. I was even hoping to take a study-abroad trip to France my senior year. That seems very unlikely at this point. I can't imagine leaving Steven with Dad for an extended period.

I want to learn Spanish now, though. Mom spoke it only a little, and she never taught me. Here in San Antonio, there are so many people who look like me who can't speak any Spanish at all. But some people outside of Texas find that peculiar. On a mother-daughter trip to New York City two summers ago, Mom and I found that most Latinos we encountered, even as young as me, spoke Spanish, and some were surprised that we weren't fluent. I'm hoping that Señora Dominguez will help me change that.

I see David again in fourth period. We're both in a class called COOP, which stands for Child-Oriented Occupational Program. It's a small class, available only to juniors who want to go into teaching or counseling. Ms. Mesa asks each of us to talk about our career goals and plans. I explain that I want to major in art education and possibly teach in a high school or at the university level one day.

That's what I've been saying for years whenever someone asked what I wanted to be or do when I grow up. When I was at Austin PFA, it seemed obvious. But that whole plan, the plan for my life I carefully structured, is so uncertain now.

The girl sitting next to me, Makaila Thomas, says she loves science and wants to be a high school chemistry teacher, which is beyond my comprehension. I can't understand why anyone would willingly take more science classes than needed and then compound that by teaching it as a career. But since Makaila is literally wearing a T-shirt with *STEMinist* emblazoned on it, it's clear that she feels differently.

When it's David's turn, he says he loves sports and wants to be a PE teacher and a coach. Another kid, Carlos, says he basically wants to do the same thing, but I think David sounds more passionate about it. Maybe he's the kind of person who just seems enthusiastic about everything. Kind of like Mom.

That evening, I make my mom's chicken enchiladas, following the handwritten recipe on an index card. She has two enchilada recipes in her little wooden recipe box. One of them is for Mexican enchiladas, and the other is for Guatemalan enchiladas. Mom's grandfather Eugenio was born in Guatemala. During

Guatemala's thirty-six-year civil war, he moved to Mexico City where he met my great-grandma Maria. My mom would sometimes make the Guatemalan enchiladas, but they're so different from the Mexican enchiladas all Texans know. The Mexican chicken enchiladas are the ones we're more used to, and that particular index card has some major red sauce stains on it. I stare at my mom's handwriting for a full ten minutes as they bake in the oven.

Dad eats in his room in his recliner with the bottle of Scotch secured between his legs. Actually, I think it's a different bottle. He must've finished the original one and gone to the liquor store for a replacement.

Steven pleads to eat at the coffee table while he watches the Astros play. Usually I resist his pleas and we eat together at the kitchen table. Today I give in, too tired to argue with him. I eat in the kitchen, reading a chapter in my physics book to prepare for tomorrow's quiz. I aced today's quiz thanks to David's mostly decipherable notes. I take my eyes off the page for a second as I let myself remember his brown eyes.

He noticed me yesterday; he sought me out today. He didn't have to do that, but he did, which creates dozens of questions in my head. Questions that will probably persist in my brain later when I'm trying to sleep.

I toss aside my book—it will have to wait. I check my phone, and there's a text from Alexa.

ALEXA: How's your first week so far? Miss you.

SARAH: Not great. I cut classes the first day already.

ALEXA: What? Why? You never cut.

SARAH: My dad.

ALEXA: (Hugs) I'm so sorry. You shouldn't have to be dealing with that. How's school otherwise?

SARAH: Meh. It's okay. How's everything there?
ALEXA: Only okay. Not great without you.

In the three months since I left Austin, I've tried to keep in touch with people from PFA, but most of those friendships have fizzled out. Alexa is the only one I regularly text anymore. She's from San Antonio too; we've been friends since third grade when we both bonded over hating PE. Whenever our class had to run laps around the perimeter of the school, Alexa and I would trail at the very end until everyone else had lapped us several times. We went to middle school together and then both applied to Austin PFA. Her focus is dance while mine is art. Was art.

We text back and forth for a few more minutes, and I almost tell her about David and his extremely brown eyes, but I don't. I don't want to make a big deal of it.

I gather the dishes from the table and bring them to the sink. As I wash them, I turn my neck from side to side, trying to stretch out all the kinks that have accumulated from the day. My hands are in the sudsy water scrubbing a pan. I feel the weight of the week's events on my shoulders. These stressors are not going away; they are a part of my life. I accept that, but it doesn't make it any easier to deal with them.

Dad comes in with his dishes and puts them in the sink. He leans back against the counter and stares at the floor. His stubble is starting to creep in.

"I'm really sorry about yesterday, Sarah," he says, his eyes still fixed on the floor.

I'm so tired of these apologies. They never lead to any change. They're just his way of avoiding a conflict, a confrontation. Sometimes it seems like he isn't even speaking to me; he's just saying the words by rote.

Over these last six months, I haven't ever felt as if he's fully paying attention to me. He's been so caught up in his own grief, he hasn't been able to look outside it—not even to comfort us, his kids who lost their mom. From day one when he had Vic call me instead of calling me himself, my dad has been alone in his sorrow, forcing Steven and me to be alone in ours.

"I think you should look into the therapist Vic told you about." I hand him the card Vic put on the refrigerator almost a month ago.

He holds the card in his hands and nods. "Yeah, that's a good idea. Maybe that will help." He puts it on the table and picks up the envelope from his mutual fund company, which I left on the kitchen table this morning. "I guess I'll go to bed now. I'm pretty tired."

I can't say goodnight, so I just watch him as he walks away, opening the letter. He's probably trying to figure out how long this latest disbursement will last.

I think about calling Vic. I haven't told him what happened yesterday. Vic can only do so much, though. Dad is the one who has to decide to see the therapist.

And if he doesn't, I can't see a way out of this. Even if we could afford for me to go back to PFA for senior year, I can't imagine leaving Steven here with him.

CHAPTER THREE

Friday night. In Texas, those words are synonymous with football—high school football. Stadiums around the state fill to capacity. It isn't just high school students and their families. People with no affiliation to a school go to the games too. It's just what Texans do from August to December, and our family is no exception. I would like to be an exception, but I don't have that luxury because of Steven.

Steven loves everything about football. For him, especially, it's all about the numbers. Jersey numbers. Yardage numbers. Downs. Points. Stats.

When I was in Austin, Mom and Dad took him to the games. Now the task is mine. I asked Dad if he wanted to come, but he said maybe next time. This is the first game of the season, will be the first game without Mom. Probably too much for him to face.

Steven always sits in the same seat—east side, fifty-yard line, ten rows up, ten seats in. We've only been here a few minutes before Steven decides he wants popcorn. He's old enough, he's contended many times, to get his own snacks, so I stay to save our seats while he goes to the concession stand.

As I watch him over my shoulder, I find myself looking into David Garza's deep brown eyes. He's coming down the bleacher steps with two guys right behind him. The dimpled smile he throws in my direction is followed by a wave. I wave back and attempt a smile. He stops in the aisle for a moment and turns around to talk to his friends. I know one of them, and he knows me, but we don't make eye contact. They continue down the aisle and find seats a few rows in front of me.

David stops in my row and sits down next to me. "Hi, Sarah."

"Hello," I say and throw another look behind me for Steven.

"So, are you a big football fan?"

"Jeez, no," I say, eyeing the seat that Steven vacated and David has seized. "I'm here with someone."

David closes his eyes and sighs. "Of course. You're with someone."

"Why are you in my seat?" Steven's question startles David and he jumps to his feet.

"Sorry." He eyes Steven, who quickly sits down and digs his hand into his popcorn.

I suppress a smile. "David, this is my brother, Steven. Steven, David."

"Who are you?" Steven asks.

"I'm David Garza, from Sarah's physics class."

"You go to Richards?"

David sits down in the empty seat next to Steven. "Yes, I do. So, you're the football fan in the family?"

"Yeah. I love football. Who's your pro team? Cowboys or Texans?"

"The 'boys, of course," David says.

"Good answer." Steven holds up a hand for a high five.

David looks over at me and smiles. He's clearly pleased with himself for winning over my little brother.

Steven watches the activity on the field, his eyes darting from one player to another. I can almost see the numbers flash in his mind. He spots a jersey number, matches it to a name, and then thinks about the player's height and weight.

"See number forty-two?" Steven asks David, pointing toward a player on the field who's caught a pass. "That's Marcus Rodriguez. He's six feet, four inches tall, and he weighs a hundred ninety-two pounds."

David acknowledges the information with a slight nod.

"And number sixty-five is Jared White. He's six-two and two hundred seventy-five pounds."

"He's an offensive tackle. They have to be big guys," David says.

"Yeah, and number fifty-nine is six-four, two hundred twenty pounds." Steven keeps rattling off numbers. "You see the quarterback? His name is Charlie Evers. He's five-eleven and weighs one ninety-five."

"One ninety-five. That's good. He's bulked up a little. Last year when he was a junior, he only weighed like one eighty-eight. He probably spent the summer lifting weights. It sounds like he grew about an inch too."

"Yes! Last year he was only five-nine."

I sit up in my seat and look at David. He just carried on a conversation with Steven about how much the guy weighs? Is he serious? Does he actually care?

"Do you know how much the defensive tackle, number fifty-two, weighs?" David asks Steven about a huge player who stands on the sidelines.

"Jacob Jones. He weighs two eighty-five."

"No way! Man, two eighty-five." David shakes his head. "He's only a junior. Next year he might even be bigger."

"My dad says defensive tackles have to be big if they're going to go after the other team's quarterback," notes Steven.

"For sure. How do you know so much about the players?" David asks.

"I look on the internet."

"Right. Well, you are quite a fan. I don't think I know anyone who knows so much about this team."

Steven looks away from the field and beams at David. When he turns his bright smile to me, I smile back.

CHAPTER FOUR

Monday comes with a vengeance as Mondays often do. The weekend went by too quickly and was filled with unrestful activities. I was hoping for a little bit of TV binging or FaceTiming Alexa, but homework, keeping up with the Etsy projects, and grocery shopping with Steven filled most of those two days.

In first period, I'm reading over my notes, wondering what David's notes for the same day look like. I saved the picture I took of his notes that second day of school. I don't need them anymore, but I like to look at them sometimes. I like to study his handwriting, the messy way he writes the letters, the way he never crosses his *t*'s.

"Good morning," David says, sliding into the desk next to me.

"Hi."

He sweeps his bangs to the side and leans forward. "I really liked meeting your brother."

"I hope he didn't bore you with all those stats."

"I don't mind." Kindness tugs at the corners of his eyes. "Does he play sports?"

"No. He prefers to watch."

"He's a neat kid. Is he your only brother?"

"Yeah."

"Well, thanks for letting me sit with you guys. I had fun." He means well; I don't know why this conversation is bothering me. It's something about the way he's entered my personal life without permission. Steven and I don't need an interloper trying to understand us.

"Can I ask you something?" I say.

David nods.

"All those heights and weights you and Steven were talking about? Do you really care about that stuff?"

"Sure. It's part of the game. The size of the players is important in football."

"Yeah, but to know the actual numbers—that's not something most football fans know, right?"

He shrugs. "The exact numbers, maybe not. Rough estimates are what most people talk about. It's pretty amazing that he can remember the exact heights and weights from just seeing them on the internet."

"Yeah. His rote memory is of encyclopedic proportions." I roll my pen over my desk. "No one has had that type of conversation with him before and found it interesting."

"Maybe he's just been talking to the wrong people," David says with a wink as he turns around to face Mr. Lemmon at the front of the room.

I can't suppress a smile. So, David is the right people—is that what he's saying?

Ms. Mesa, our COOP teacher, is my favorite at Richards High. She's in her late fifties and has been teaching high school for thirty-five years. During that time she's taught English, language arts, psychology, and sociology. She's told us that this is her favorite class because she gets to help prepare future teachers.

Today, she hands us permission slips and passes around a sign-up sheet. "In October, we'll start visiting Las Positas Elementary School. We'll observe different classrooms in grades one through five—all subjects, including PE, music, art. Eventually, each of you will lead a class in your chosen subject area, which you can mark on the sign-up sheet going around. So, get these permission slips signed because we'll be taking little field trips two to three times per week."

I look at the parent/guardian signature line on the paper. I want to laugh out loud at the thought of asking my dad to sign it. Somehow his signature is required to allow me to attend off-campus events even though I'm the reason he has three meals a day, clean clothes, and working electricity.

I think about all that Mom did for me, for us, all of my life. She wanted me to focus on school and my art, but my focus now is on making sure Dad and Steven eat every day. She would especially hate what I have to do with the Etsy shop—drawing for profit, rather than for personal fulfillment.

"Are you going to the football game on Friday?" David asks me the next day as we're leaving physics.

I laugh. That isn't really a choice for me. "Steven never misses one, so I'll be there too."

"I might be a little late. Will you save me a seat?"

I look away and think about it for a moment. "Sure. We always sit in the same seats."

"Thanks," he says. "Have a good day."

The rest of the day is fine. I wouldn't call it a *good* day; it's just fine. I've met a few people in my classes, but so far I've sat with someone different at lunch every day. I don't even think I remember any of their names. Home still feels like Austin PFA to me. I keep having to remind myself that I am not going back. I'm here now.

Fifteen minutes. Every day, I have fifteen minutes to breathe, to not feel responsible for the lives of others. That's how long it takes for me to pull out of my parking spot, follow the slow line of drivers all desperate to see Richards High in their rearview mirror, and reach home.

For fifteen minutes, I can turn myself off and turn music up. It takes those fifteen minutes to restore my sanity, to refill my depleting well of patience. When I pull into the driveway at home, I have to be on again. Dealing with Dad is mentally exhausting and is becoming a new and different challenge every day.

I find Steven at the kitchen table doing his spelling homework. I grab a banana and a bottle of water and sit down next to him, thinking about the therapist's card on the refrigerator. Should I bring it up again or will that make Dad even more defiant, more reluctant to go?

Dad walks out of the home office he and Mom shared, which is just off the kitchen. He hasn't been in there much in the last few months, so it startles me to see him emerging from it now. His desk and computer have been abandoned, his bookshelves gathering dust. On the other side of the room, my mom's side, her desk is still cluttered with notebooks and textbooks. She was a professor at UTSA too. She taught classes in Latin American studies. I've been wanting to go in there, to scour through her journals, to see her writing, to find out what she was thinking the last few days before she died, but I'm not ready yet. Every time I look in the room, I stare at her chair and remember seeing her curly black hair running down the back of that chair as she swiveled from side to side.

Dad places a computer printout on the table between Steven and me. "I just bought us cruise tickets to Central and South America. We can finally take that vacation she always wanted us to have."

"What do you mean, cruise tickets?" I ask, grabbing the paper.

"We leave next week. You know she wanted us to do this; she'd been planning it. And now we need to do it—finally."

I scan the dates and the ticket prices. "Next week? This is ridiculous. School just started."

"I know, but this is a good reason to miss. Maybe it will help us all, doing something she wanted us to."

He's looking for answers somewhere he can't find them. A cruise won't make him start living again. He needs real therapy from professionals who know how to help people who are going through what he's going through.

"We can't." I slam the paper down, jolting my water bottle. "We can't just leave. Steven doesn't even have a passport! Besides, this is too expensive. It's a nice idea, but it isn't going to solve our problems. Maybe one day, when you're better, when we can afford it."

He crosses his arms. "Sarah, I still make some of the decisions around here. I think this will really be good for us."

I get up, pushing my chair back. "Did you see how much it costs? That money could go a long way toward paying for your treatment. Mom would . . . she would want you to get better. That would be more important to her than a cruise to South America."

"You don't understand." He shakes his head but looks uncertain now.

"Mom doesn't like it when you two fight," Steven says, not looking up from his spelling homework.

Dad picks up the printout. "I'm going to take a look into getting Steven that passport."

"Come on, Dad. Passports take weeks." I turn my back to him and open the refrigerator to figure out what to make for dinner.

"I'm sure there's a way to expedite it," Dad says.

"Sure, Dad. You look into that. Go ahead!" I slam the refrigerator door closed and walk to the dishwasher.

Wordlessly, Dad leaves the room, and I hear him go upstairs.

"Mom doesn't like it when you talk back, Sarah," Steven says.

I open the dishwasher, thinking about the conversation I want to have with Dad about the therapist. Clearly, this was not the right time to bring it up. He's probably still clutching the printout of the cruise itinerary, seated in his recliner, filling his empty stomach with Scotch. It was probably the damn History Channel showing some documentary about Guatemala that even put the idea into his head.

I start unloading the dishwasher. With each spoon that I set in the silverware drawer, I use increasing force, and soon I'm just hurling them at the drawer, one after the other. I slam the drawer shut and it comes rolling back out, mocking me. The top drawer of the dishwasher holds two Tupperware containers, and I grab them with tight fists. When I open the cabinet, some bowls come tumbling down to the floor. I shove the containers in, banging the door shut.

I go out to the hallway where Steven can't see me and sink to the floor. Pulling my knees into my chest, I sit there, heavy breaths coming with each rise of my shoulders. I reach out to touch the oak table, running my fingertips against the smooth cherry-colored wood. Mom brought it home one day, salvaged it from the side of the road. She stripped it, sanded it, and refinished it.

Atop the long, thin tabletop is a red-framed picture of Mom and Steven. Mom's black curly hair, streaming behind her, shines in the afternoon sun. In the picture, Steven is five, and Mom is pushing him on a swing at the park. He's holding tightly to the chains of the swing, his feet clutched together, and there's a look of uncertainty in his face.

Next to that frame is an oval ceramic frame with a photo of eight-year-old me holding Steven in my mom's hospital room the day he was born. He was a fussy baby; he cried constantly and was difficult to soothe. I held him for hours in the hospital room, rocking him back and forth until the crying subsided. Anytime I heard Steven crying, I'd go to Mom's side and ask to hold him. I wanted to be the one to make the crying stop. Mom let me soothe him a lot, but she was the expert. A whisper, a kiss, a touch—anything from Mom calmed Steven.

There are other pictures of Steven and me all over the house, but these two were Mom's favorites.

I melt onto the hallway floor, stifling my sobs as I think about my brother calmly doing his homework in the other room, and about my dad upstairs, trying to get him a passport for a trip that will never happen.

CHAPTER FIVE

In Texas, September still feels like summer, especially with bodies crammed together for a football game. The players on the field are warming up, getting ready for the game to start. Wearing the pads and helmets must make it feel twenty degrees hotter. I pull up my hair and twist it around twice before banding it together with an elastic. What is the point of having long hair if I'm always pulling it up?

I asked Dad to come tonight. He said he wanted to clean out the garage. He's been laser-focused on that ever since he canceled the cruise. The golf clubs and tools he cleaned the other day are gone. He probably sold them or pawned them. How much money do we have left? How many of his things will he sell off if he wants to buy more Scotch?

Steven sits beside me, pointing randomly at players, reciting their heights and weights. I wipe my sweaty hands on my shorts and pick up my cold water bottle. I take a drink and then rub it on my forehead, savoring the coolness against my skin.

"Hi," David says, coming down the row toward us. He takes the seat next to me and leans forward to greet Steven.

"Hi," Steven says, turning to look at him.

"You're on time," I say. "You said you would be late."

He smiles. His skin glistens in the hot lights of the stadium.

"I know. I just said that so you'd save me a seat."

I shake my head. "So, you're a liar, basically, is what you're saying."

He adjusts his baseball cap. "I'm sorry I lied, Sarah. You're not really mad, are you?"

"Whatever. Why do you want to sit next to us?"

"Well, school is so busy, we don't get a chance to talk very much. You don't mind if I sit by you, do you?" David asks.

I shrug. "No. You can sit here. I'm sorry I don't know enough about football to make stimulating conversation."

"That's why Steven's here, right?" David leans slightly across me. He's not touching me, but he's in my space enough that I breathe in the faint scent of aftershave or something. I look at the side of his face, shaved and smooth. "Steven, do you have a favorite player?" he asks.

"Bobby Mendoza, number twenty-two," Steven says, pointing to the field.

"Bobby's good. He's a friend of mine. We went to elementary together."

"Really?"

David nods. "Yeah. I talk to him all the time. He's a good guy, really good guy. He's being recruited by UT, UCLA—but he doesn't let any of that go to his head."

"Does he like baseball?" Steven asks, taking his eyes off the field to look at David.

"Loves it. Why? Do you like baseball?"

Steven turns back to the field. "Yeah, it's my favorite sport besides football."

"What's your team?"

"The Houston Astros." He pulls up his sleeve to show David one of my Sharpie tattoos, the Astros logo on his bicep.

"Wow!" David says, leaning over me a little more to look at Steven's arm. The side of David's head is right at my eye level, and I stare at the faint glow of his light brown skin. Without moving his head, David turns his eyes to the side to catch me staring at him. He sits back in his seat and asks, "Is that a fake tattoo?"

"Sarah drew it," Steven says, not taking his eyes off the field. He rolls his sleeve back down.

"You drew that?" he asks me.

"It's Sharpie," I say.

"That's amazing work," David says. He leans forward again, talking to Steven. "I like the Astros too. Lifelong fan. My dad used to take me to games all the time when I was a kid."

Steven bounces up in his seat. "My dad used to take me to games when I was a kid too. He doesn't anymore." He turns back to the field. "He doesn't do anything anymore. He just stays in his room all day."

"I'm sorry," David says. He looks at me, and I turn my head toward Steven. "Is he sick?"

Steven shrugs. "I don't know. Is he sick, Sarah?"

"Something like that," I say, watching the cheerleaders.

David sits up and crosses his arms. "Well, if your dad says it's okay, I can take you to a game sometime, Steven."

"Really?" Steven's head shoots toward David, and he leans across me. "Is that okay, Sarah?"

I watch Steven's pleading face—his eyebrows knit together, his eyes scrunched. "Please, Sarah. Please, can I go?" He interlocks his fingers and waves his clasped hands in front of my face. "Please."

I sigh and look at David, who shrugs and makes an apologetic face. I turn back to Steven. "I don't know. We'll have to see."

"Come on, Sarah. You know Dad won't care. Why are you saying no?"

"I didn't say no. I said we'll see."

Steven crosses his arms and turns to watch the game. "*We'll see* means no," he says to no one in particular.

David leans over and whispers into my ear. His lips tickle and I shiver. "I'm so sorry."

I pull away from him and force a smile. "That's okay."

"I really don't mind taking him. I haven't been to a game in a long time."

"I guess I'm the bad guy if I say no. I'd have two people hating me."

"Oh, I would never hate you," David says with a wink.

My forced smile evolves into an authentic one. I know Steven would enjoy the trip; it's probably exactly what he needs. "Well, okay."

"Good! It will be fun. You'll see. You're coming, right?"

"Of course. I wouldn't let Steven go alone." I'll have to ask Vic to stay with Dad. I can't leave him by himself.

"Maybe we'll turn you into a baseball fan." David leans across me again and pats Steven on the shoulder. "She said yes. We can go."

"Really? Sarah, really?"

"Yes." I nod, pleased with his smile. There aren't many things that prompt genuine smiles from Steven these days.

"When are we going?"

"I'll look into tickets," David says. "Maybe for a Saturday game. Playoffs are coming up, so it'll have to be soon. Do you guys have anything planned for Saturdays this month?"

"No," I say. We rarely do anything on Saturdays anymore.

"Who do you think they'll play?" Steven asks David.

"Maybe the Texas Rangers, or the New York Yankees, or the Oakland A's."

"I don't know," David says. "I'll look at a schedule, and maybe text Sarah." He looks at me and raises an eyebrow.

"Does that mean I have to give you my phone number now?"

He nods. "I think so."

Steven calls out my number and David hurries to program it into his phone.

CHAPTER SIX

As I head toward my car after school on Monday, I catch sight of David walking with Brad. They're near my parked car, so I slow down.

Almost as if David can sense me staring at the back of his head, the broad expanse of his shoulders, and his neatly combed straight hair, he turns around, spots me and stops. By default, Brad also stops, the familiar smirk returning. I want to slow my pace even more so I don't catch up with them, but they're both looking straight at me.

"Hey, Sarah," David says, blocking the sun out of his eyes with one hand.

"Hi, Sarah," Brad says, mimicking David's tone.

I turn my eyes away from David's inviting smile to face Brad. "There are three thousand people at this school. Why are you talking to me?"

I don't miss the confused look on David's face as Brad shakes his head. "When are you going to grow up?"

"Just walk away from me, Brad."

"Uh, what's going on?" David asks, looking from Brad to me.

Brad ignores David. "You're still the same petty person."

David grabs Brad's arm. "What the hell, man?"

"Don't waste your time with her," says Brad.

"You're the one getting in her face. What's wrong with you?"

Instead of answering, Brad turns around and walks away.

"What just happened?" David asks me.

I start toward my car again. "Brad is a jerk. How did a semi-nice guy like you end up with him as a friend?"

"We play basketball together. I take it there's history between you two? I didn't know. I've never seen him act like that before." He walks me the rest of the way to my car. "Did he do something to you?"

"Brad used to be my friend. We were pretty close up until I gave him a black eye in sixth grade."

David tries to suppress a smile. "How did that happen?"

I don't know why I just blurted that out. The backstory of the black eye is not something I ever planned to disclose to a near-stranger. But there was something revealing about the way David grabbed Brad's arm and called him out just now. A lot of people would've frozen up, or tried to ignore how Brad was acting, or pretended it wasn't a big deal. David's more than just a cute guy; he's a guy who pays attention, a guy who cares about the truth and about other people. The kind of person I can trust.

"Brad was my first kiss. But when he kissed me, he also put his hand up my shirt. We were in sixth grade! Every girl wants her first kiss to be sweet, special, memorable. No girl alive wants a guy to stick his hand up her shirt on the first kiss. You wouldn't do that, would you?" I look up at him.

He shakes his head. "No way. I wouldn't do that."

"See? So, of course I had to punch him." I reach to my back pocket and take out my phone. I show David my phone case, which is decorated with a reproduction of Gustav Klimt's famous painting, *The Kiss*. "Look at where his hands are—they're framing her face. She's in complete bliss from his hands on her face, his lips on her cheek. That is how a girl wants to be kissed."

David takes my phone and studies the picture. "And you speak for all girls?"

"All rational girls," I say, grabbing my phone from him.

David smiles. "I'm glad you gave me this insight. I will definitely remember it the next time I'm ready to kiss someone." He watches me intently, and I try to keep eye contact with him, but my gaze disobediently strays down to his mouth.

I quickly turn toward my car. "I think I'd better go."

"I'm really sorry about Brad. I didn't know he was like that."

I shrug. "It's not your fault. It was a long time ago, but I don't think he's changed."

"I'll keep that in mind. So, I looked at tickets for the Astros game. Can you and Steven go this Saturday?"

"Yeah, I think that should work. Just let me know how much I owe you for the tickets."

"Don't worry about it," he says.

"Of course I have to pay for our tickets."

"Hey, I'm trying to be a semi-nice guy here."

I smile. "I'm sorry I said that. I didn't mean it. Talking to Brad just threw me off. You're definitely a three-fourths-nice guy. But I am paying for the tickets for Steven and me."

"Okay, I'll text you later." He smiles as he walks away.

Conjugating Spanish verbs has become my new nemesis. I've been staring at the same page in my textbook for half an hour when Dad walks into the kitchen with his laptop and sits down next to me at the table. I hope he isn't looking for any more cruise tickets. At least he was able to get a partial refund for the booking he canceled.

He puts his reading glasses on and starts to type. I watch him for a minute. "What are you working on?"

"I need to start publishing articles again," he says without looking up. It's been too long since I heard him mention publishing. Part of me wants to peer over his shoulder to see if the article he's drafting is even coherent. At one point, he wrote well-researched and eloquent pieces for respected historical journals, and I just hope this is for real.

I close my Spanish textbook because I really don't even understand what pretérito is. "I'm so glad to see you feel like working. I'd love to read it when you're done."

"Maybe," he says, glancing at me for an instant.

Since he's lucid and focused on something good, this might be the right time to bring up the therapist. "Can I call that therapist tomorrow and make an appointment for you?"

He looks up from his laptop. "No, Sarah. That's really not necessary."

"I think it is."

"I'm doing so much better now. I'm working and pretty soon I can get my job back. I just don't think I need to spend the money on a therapist."

I stop myself from pointing out that it'd be much better to spend money on therapy than on booze or impulse buys. "I still think you should do it. Sometimes therapists have reduced rates if you don't have insurance. We should call the one on the card that Vic gave you."

Instead of answering, he stands up, slams the laptop closed, and walks into the home office.

I think about the other times he's said he was doing better, about the day or two at a time when he's seemed like he was back to normal, back to the dad I knew. But it never sticks, because as soon as the next wave of sadness hits him, he falls apart again. Retreats, starts drinking, abandons whatever he seemed enthusiastic about before. By tomorrow, he'll be back to more Scotch.

I pull my backpack across the floor toward me and shove the Spanish textbook inside. I think about studying for the physics quiz or working on an English essay that's due soon, but I can't care about either of those at the moment. I take out my Sharpies and choose a deep purple one. I turn over my left arm and start drawing a long-stemmed tulip on my forearm. I use thin strokes for the stem, coloring it in with a rich green Sharpie. I work on the drawing until Steven ambles into the kitchen wondering what's for dinner.

Dinner is the absolute last thing on my mind, behind Dad's supposed writing, the unmade therapy appointment, the impossible Spanish verbs, the unfinished drawing of Skipper and her freckles, the streaking of the pink on my Sharpie tulip, and the question of why David hasn't texted yet.

"I don't know, Steven. Maybe just have some cereal."

"Yes!" Steven says with a substantial amount of enthusiasm that leads me to believe he's getting tired of my cooking. "Can I eat it in the living room?"

"Sure," I say. "Whatever." I leave Steven in the kitchen trying to carry the milk carton, bowl, spoon, and box of Cheerios all in one trip.

In my room, I text Vic to see if he can stay with Dad when Steven and I go to the Astros game. Vic says he and Laura will come over with some meat to grill and maybe convince

Dad to watch the game on TV with them. I thank him with ten grateful-hands emojis and finally pull out Skipper's picture. I'm already two days past the promised delivery date, and there is currently an unanswered email in my inbox from Skipper's mom.

My phone buzzes with a text, and I'm grateful for the reprieve from worrying about how I'm going to respond to that email. I assume the text is from Alexa because she's really the only one who texts me anymore.

It's from David, and I drop Skipper's picture to read it.

DAVID: Hi, Sarah. I can't wait for Saturday. Here are the tickets.

Looking at the screenshot he's sent, I quickly do the math in my head to figure out how much it will cost for Steven and me. I check my account to see how much I have. Not much, but I can at least pay for the tickets.

SARAH: Thank you. Can I Cash App you the money?

DAVID: Nah, don't worry about it. We can talk about it Saturday.

SARAH: Okay, I can give you cash on Saturday.

DAVID: Tell Steven we're playing the Mariners. It's gonna be a good matchup.

SARAH: Thank you! He'll be so excited.

DAVID: I'm excited too. Have a good night.

SARAH: Good night.

I wait a few minutes to see if he's going to text anything else, but he doesn't. I FaceTime Alexa and tell her every detail about David, starting with his messy notes.

Alexa and I have about ten minutes of overlap in our lunch periods each day. So I sit at a picnic table in the courtyard to FaceTime her while we eat.

"What are you eating today?" she asks me, showing me her pasta salad.

"Turkey sandwich." I hold it up for her to see before I take a bite.

"Nice. Speaking of turkey, I'm definitely coming home for Thanksgiving, so we can hang out then."

"That's great." I can't imagine Thanksgiving without my mom, but I don't say that. No point in spoiling Alexa's excitement.

"And maybe you can come up to Austin for the Winter Spectacular the week before Christmas," she goes on. "There'll be musical numbers. The orchestra is doing a whole thing. I'm dancing a scene from *The Nutcracker*."

"I'd love to come, if I can bring Steven with me. I don't want to leave him here."

"My parents are going, so you can ride with them. I'll talk to them."

"That would be perfect. I definitely don't want to miss it," I say, remembering when I participated in PFA's Winter Spectacular. I did some snowy watercolor displays for the stage, and I designed the cover of the program.

Alexa puts down her phone and tightens the high ponytail holding up her straight black hair. "I have to go to class in a minute."

"I'm glad we got to talk for a little bit. I miss you so much."

"I'll have to call you tonight to tell you about what the heck is going on in orchestra."

"Hey, Sarah." A voice nearby. It's David, carrying a mini

carton of milk in one hand and some napkin-wrapped apple slices in the other. He sits down on the bench next to me. "Oh, sorry. I didn't realize you were on FaceTime."

"That's okay," I say, angling the phone toward him. "Alexa has to go in a minute."

Alexa peers in closer. "Is that David?" she asks.

David looks from Alexa to me. "Wait, did you tell her about me?"

Alexa makes a face, knowing she just let something slip. "Hi, I'm Alexa Alvarez. I'm Sarah's friend from PFA."

"PFA?" he asks.

"My old school," I say.

David smiles and leans in to face Alexa. "Hi, Alexa. It's nice to meet you. So, what did Sarah say about me?"

Alexa shrugs. "Sorry, I have to go. I can't be late for class. Bye!" She ends the call.

"She seems nice," David says to me. "Sorry I interrupted. I just wanted to see what time you want to leave tomorrow."

We agree to leave at nine in the morning, since the drive is almost four hours, and I text him our address. While I finish my sandwich, he takes a final gulp from his milk carton and eats an apple slice. "Want part of a caramel apple?" he asks. "One of the PTA moms was giving out samples in the cafeteria. They're good but I've probably had enough."

He offers me the napkin, which holds a chunk of a candied apple. I accept his offering and take a bite. "Does the PTA regularly give out free snacks?"

"Nah, they're just showing off what they're going to sell at the fall festival in October. Trying to lure in future customers."

"Well, it'll probably work. This is tasty." I've seen flyers for the festival on various bulletin boards around school, but I

44

haven't given it any thought. In fact, I've probably spent more time thinking about the PFA events and traditions that I'm missing out on. Maybe I'll duck into the cafeteria at the end of lunch and check out the rest of the samples.

"I really like that flower," David says, pointing to the tulip on my arm. "Did you draw that?"

"Yeah, with Sharpie." I'm glad he doesn't notice the imperfections that frustrated me last night.

"I would really like one of those Astros logos you did on Steven. You think you could draw one for me before the game tomorrow?"

I look down at the smooth brown skin of his forearm. "Sure. I can do it right now." I pull out a small wet wipe from my bag and rip it open. When I take his arm, he easily relaxes it for me to handle. "Where, right here?" I ask, touching a promising spot with the wet wipe.

"Sure."

I pull my foot up on the bench, rest his arm on my knee, and rub the spot with the small wipe.

"I feel like I'm getting my blood drawn," he says, watching me.

"You don't have to worry about that. I hate needles, which is why I will never get a real tattoo." I lean down and blow on his arm to dry the area I just scrubbed. For a moment I wonder if he's even awake because every part of him seems still.

He lets out a small breath and I feel his arm completely relax against my knee. "So how long do these last?"

"A couple of weeks." I press down with the blue Sharpie, bracing his arm against my knee. I outline a large blue circle, and inside that an orange circle.

I blow on the marker to dry it and adjust David's arm

against my knee. With my free hand, I toss my curls over my shoulder so they don't fall in my face. I draw a large orange star in the center of the orange circle and outline a block letter *H* in the middle of the star. I alternately color orange for the star and blue for the background. I can feel David watching me. "Are you watching me?"

A wide smile spreads on his face and his eyes hold mine. "A little bit. Is that okay? It's just cool to see you work. I don't know how you can keep your hand so steady and make it so precise."

"A lot of practice, I guess." I continue alternating between orange and blue, pausing briefly to look at his fingers. They're long, and I let myself imagine, for a moment, placing my hand in his and letting him wrap his fingers securely around mine. I toss the thought away and finish coloring in the star, leaving the large *H* uncolored. "Okay. Almost done."

"Wow. That's amazing." David lifts his arm off my knee and brings it closer to his face to get a better look.

I put the markers in my backpack and take out my little bottle of baby powder. "This helps it last longer." I sprinkle a small dusting of baby powder and rub it in with my index finger.

"That kind of tickles, but I like it," David says. He's watching my finger rub across the width of his arm, and I see him swallow hard.

"Last step," I say, reaching for the travel-size bottle of hair spray I keep in my backpack. I spray two pumps on his arm.

"Very cool. I'm going to have to think of another one I want on this other arm. Do you do Batman?"

I laugh as I put away the baby powder and hair spray. "Yeah, I've done some Batmans."

"I just really like this whole process," he adds. "My arm on your leg, you blowing on my arm and rubbing the baby powder. It's just all really nice."

I liked it very much too, but I don't say that. "I'd better go. Lunch is almost over." I stand up, and David jumps to his feet.

"Okay, well, I'll see you in the morning. Thanks for the tattoo."

"You're welcome."

Right after I pull my Toyota into the driveway, I notice a car come to a stop in front of our house. I get out of my car, pulling my backpack over my shoulder, just as Vic exits the other car.

"Hey, Vic," I say.

"Hi, Sarah. Sorry it's been a while since I've been by. Things have been hectic since the semester started."

"That's okay," I say, noticing that he's carrying two plastic bags in each hand.

"Laura and I smoked a brisket, and we wanted to bring you some dinner."

I hold out my hands to take the bags. "Thank you."

He doesn't give them to me. "I'll bring this inside, so I can say hi to Steven."

I let Vic follow me into the house. Steven is at the kitchen table eating a bowl of cereal. I wonder if he thinks that's his dinner from now on just because I let him do it once.

"Vic!" Steven says, putting down his spoon.

Vic puts the bags on the table and gives Steven a high five. "How's school going so far? Third grade—it's the big time now, huh?"

"It's good. We get to have music class now. What'd you bring?"

"Brisket, potato salad, pickles, and that bread you like."

Steven looks at Vic with wide eyes. "The white bread?"

"Yeah, bud, the white bread." Our parents have always been super strict about only having whole wheat bread, and Steven loves barbeque places where white bread slices are offered with every meal.

"Thanks for bringing all of this, Vic," I say while Steven starts rummaging through the bags. "It smells delicious."

"Of course."

I sit down next to Steven, who has found the plastic baggie with the slices of white bread and is taking giant bites. "Are you still okay with checking in on Dad tomorrow?" I ask Vic. "I don't want to leave him alone all day." I want to tell him about what happened the first day of school, but I think half-truths are better for now. I'm worried that if Vic knows the whole truth he might feel, at some point, compelled to call CPS.

"Yeah, for sure," Vic says. "In fact, I was hoping to talk to him now—see if he wants to come over tomorrow or let us hang out here."

While Vic heads upstairs, Steven starts uncovering containers and digging into the brisket with his fingers. I pull off a piece of brisket and slide it into my mouth. Eventually I grab forks so we can dig into the potato salad in between picking off pieces of brisket. Steven has eaten all the white bread.

Vic comes back down after a few minutes. He pulls out a chair, sighing, and sinks down. "Your dad is a stubborn man, guys. He says he'll be fine, but I'm still going to drop in and check on him. I still have the key you gave me, Sarah. I told him Laura is making pies tomorrow, so I would bring him one."

"Did you ask him about the therapist again?"

Vic nods. "Yeah. He still says no. We'll keep working on him. Are you sure you and Steven are fine here?"

I look at Steven, who's fishing pickles out of a plastic baggie with his fingers. "Yeah, we'll be fine."

"Okay. I'll come by and check on your dad tomorrow, and I'll call you next week to see how it's going."

"Thanks, Vic. And thanks again for the food. The brisket is so good."

"Yeah, thanks, Vic," Steven echoes.

"Promise you'll call me if anything changes," Vic says, pointing at me.

I get up from my chair to walk Vic to the door. "I promise," I say, knowing that I probably won't. Vic doesn't have to know about every embarrassing and neglectful thing Dad does.

CHAPTER SEVEN

$\int$ teven and I sit on the curb in front of our house waiting for David. The air is hot enough already that perspiration is gathering behind my knees. Even with fall looming, the temperature continues to hit the nineties every day. Robert is outside Wanda's house, trimming her edges with his weed-whacker. Sweat glistens on his bare back, and I turn my head away from his orange-tanned skin. I wonder if the baseball stadium will have the roof open today, leaving us defenseless against the scorching sun.

Steven plays with the strap of his iPad cover. His iPad has four movies downloaded onto it, two for the trip there and two for the trip back, he said. He cranes his neck to get a better view of the corner where David's car will turn onto our street.

David finally arrives in his Jeep, and Steven jumps up and bounds toward him. I pick up my canvas bag filled with snacks. By the time I get in the car, Steven is already buckled in, telling David about the Astros' record against the Mariners so far this year.

"What do you have there?" David asks me, pointing to my bag.

"Snacks for the road, sandwiches for lunch."

"Sandwiches?" He turns around to Steven. "We gotta have

game dogs at the stadium for lunch. You can't go to a baseball game without having a game dog."

Steven is already queueing up the first movie on his iPad. "Sarah likes to ruin fun, David. You just have to get used to it."

I tell David, "You can have your game dog, but there's nothing wrong with packing a little nutrition into the day."

David shifts into drive and shakes his head. "Game day and nutrition don't mix. What else you got in there?"

"Cold water bottles, apples, cookies. Cookies are okay, right?"

He shrugs slightly. "Depends. What kind?"

"Oatmeal raisin," I say, pulling out a plastic bag of cookies I made last night.

"I don't know. Raisins—that's nutritious. Actually, those look really good. Can I have one?"

"If you're sure it's not going against the spirit of game day."

"Well, we're not there yet, and it's a long trip."

I open the bag and hand him a cookie. "Do you want one, Steven?"

He nods and I hand him a cookie.

"Am I ruining your fun now, Steven?" I ask as he takes a big bite.

"Sarah, you have to learn to take a joke sometimes," Steven says and puts his headphones on.

David glances in his rearview mirror at Steven and smiles. "You two are really close."

"We are. We've always been."

"How old were you when he was born?"

"Eight, and I thought I could take care of him as well as my mom." I smile at the memory. "She indulged me and let me do a lot. I just had this natural instinct to take care of him—almost too much, I think, sometimes."

"I think you're a great sister."

"Well, I've become more of a mother figure since our mom died six months ago."

"I'm sorry. I didn't know."

"It's been very hard on all of us."

"I'm sure it has. He's lucky to have you, though. How did it happen, if you don't mind me asking?"

"It was a car accident." I will say no more about it to him. Each recounting and remembering of that day is like dislodging an embedded fishhook. Any detail I share just tears a little deeper.

David sets the cruise control on the car after merging into the inside lane. "So, you said that your dad is sick. That must be hard too."

More questions I don't want to answer. He's trespassing on my emotions, things I prefer to conceal from others. I'm tempted to grab the steering wheel and turn the car around. Four hours is an infinite time to sit beside him as he interrogates me on my personal life.

"Should we listen to some music?" I ask.

"Sure. Do you have a playlist on your phone? Or we can do mine."

"Yours," I say. I don't have anything on my phone that I feel like listening to right now.

He unlocks his phone and hands it to me. "I have a little bit of everything. Some oldies, some nineties, some country, some rap, some Tejano."

"Sounds great," I say, thinking I would listen to anything to avoid talking about myself. I plug in his aux cord and press play on the first playlist I find. We listen to the first three songs in silence, and I watch the cars on the highway.

"So, Alexa is your friend from your old school. Where did you go to school before Richards?" David asks, turning down the volume on the stereo.

Clearly he's not going to let me get away with the silence I hoped for. "Austin Performing and Fine Arts Academy. It's a boarding school, so I lived there. Alexa was my roommate."

"A boarding school. They really have those?" David asks.

"Yeah. They're real."

"Did you like it there?"

"I loved it. My studies focused on art. I want to be an art teacher."

"That's cool. I want to go into teaching too, or coaching really. I'd like to coach high school basketball, but I'll probably have to start off in middle school or something and probably teach and coach. We'll see."

"Well, you're good with kids, so I could see you being a coach."

"My fantasy was to play in the NBA, but that's not going to happen, so coaching it is. I play varsity now. Maybe once the season starts, you and Steven can come watch me play."

"I don't know. Steven's got me going to the football games every Friday, and baseball today, so I think that would be overkill."

I'm glad for this safer topic of conversation. I want to keep the focus off my private life, so I ask him more questions about his post-high-school plans.

We stop once for a bathroom break and to fill the Jeep with gas. When we near Houston, traffic slows at several intervals.

David glances up into the rearview mirror. "How's Steven doing back there?"

I turn around to look at Steven. His eyes are focused on his movie. "He's just fine. He loves baseball movies."

David stifles a yawn and stretches as his foot holds the brake and releases it to keep up with the slowing traffic. "When I was a kid and we'd drive here from San Antonio, for some reason, this is the point I would always have to go to the bathroom. It didn't matter that we'd just stopped a half hour before or that we were almost there. Right here is when I would say that I had to go to the bathroom. My dad used to get so mad. He'd start swearing in Spanish. We were so close to the stadium, and I just couldn't hold it. After a while, he made us start leaving the house a half hour earlier just to account for this stop."

I laugh. "So, your dad is really into baseball?"

"Big time. He used to bring us to five or six Astros games every year. His life's dream is to have season tickets, but it's too far of a drive to try to make it to all the games. He says that when he retires he'll buy a condo in Houston and go to every game. He has almost twenty-five years before he retires, so we'll see. And I'm sure my mom will have something to say about it."

I pull out a cookie and nibble on it.

"Steven said your dad is a big baseball fan too?"

I shrug and swallow the bite. "Used to be. He still watches the games sometimes, but he doesn't follow it as much anymore."

"My dad was determined to make one of us a baseball player. A major league pitcher, preferably. He made me and my brothers play Little League every year. Baseball camp every summer. He was kind of mad when I stopped playing after freshman year."

"Did you guys enjoy it?" As he talks, my eyes stray down to the Astros logo I drew on his arm, the orange and blue blending together. I remember holding his arm, resting it on my lap as I drew the delicate circles and lines.

"I did when I was little, but I didn't want to play after freshman year. I think my oldest brother got tired of it in middle school. Band was more his thing. He plays the drums in the marching band at UT. Hates sports, just wants to play drums. He and my dad went back and forth on that. But my little brother, Sam, is still doing the Little League thing."

"I bet your dad loves that. Does he go watch his games?"

"Almost every one." He pauses. "I'm sorry. I just keep going on and on about my family. You're probably getting tired of hearing about them."

I shake my head. "No, it's fine."

"Well, I wouldn't mind hearing more about *your* family." He looks over at me. "But I get the impression that you'd rather I just keep talking about mine."

"Exactly," I say as I shove the rest of the cookie into my mouth.

David smiles. "Okay, then. Let me tell you about the trip we took to Yellowstone when I was ten."

"Go ahead," I say, laughing.

We keep chatting while we exit the freeway, find a place to park, and walk several blocks to the stadium with Steven. The sunlight is weighty today, sending rays of its heat along every inch of my body.

I buy Steven a program and we find our seats. Steven sits between David and me, which is fine, because any more proximity to David would be unnerving, and currently I am trying to squash my inclination to reach out and run my fingers over the orange and blue on his smooth skin.

David looks over to me and smiles, adjusts the brim of his Astros hat. I smile back, grateful that my sunglasses are hiding the admiration that's probably sparkling right through my eyes. I turn away from him and scan the swelling crowd. Steven is leafing through the program, looking for the numbers that will merit the four-hour trip.

It's been more than a year since I've been here. We all came for Steven's birthday the June before last. It's never been my favorite pastime, to sit for nine innings watching a procession of repetitive actions—pitching, swinging the bat, running, catching balls, and switching sides. Sure, once in a while something happens. There will be an occasional hit, maybe a homerun, a close play at home. And if luck prevails, there will be a winner after nine innings. Extra innings—something that always thrilled Dad and Steven—are not my favorite.

It isn't as if I hate baseball. I grew up on it: a game on TV most nights and weekends during the season, occasional overnight trips to Houston with my family. Dad, an ardent fan, would fix his eyes on the game, taking in every pitch. And Steven, as young as three or four, would watch the large scoreboard, taking in each change in numbers, almost oblivious to the occurrences on the field. With time, he learned that a third strike would change the board, add a number to the outs column. A player crossing home would add to the runs, a ball hit over the far outfield wall might even change the runs category multiple times. A well-hit ball with a player reaching first base would cause the hits tally to increase by one.

Mom was more a fan of the experience than of the game itself. She sang along with the national anthem, drawing stares from the crowd. Often, she would attempt to start the wave, but it never proved successful. During the seventh-inning stretch, she would stand on her seat and sing the loudest.

She loved the crowd, the atmosphere, the noise, the smell, the food. A game was not complete to her without the requisite hot dog, peanuts, large drink, and cotton candy. To her, the cotton candy alone was worth the price of admission. She and I would share it, pulling pieces off, one by one, until it was gone. I would put it in my mouth and let it melt on my tongue, savoring each sweet taste, made sweeter by sharing it with my mother.

I wanted to be like my mother in every way. Happy, alive, vivacious. It didn't seem like a coincidence to me that Mom's name was Viviana, like the adjective that described her. She enjoyed each game, often leaving without even knowing the score, but with a full and fun experience. That's what mattered to her—how it was experienced, not who won.

For me, it was the love of my family that brought me to each game. Being with them shaped my life. Being at my mother's side as much as possible, absorbing her lively spirit, her perpetual happiness, was what counted for me.

This is our first Astros game since she died. Steven seems unfazed by it. After all, the numbers on the scoreboard are still there. The numbers continue without her, give him the sameness he requires. For me, it feels all wrong. The game is not right without my mother's curly hair tucked into an Astros hat, without a failed attempt at the wave, without a shared cotton candy. I look at a vendor walking down the aisle beside us. No. I can't have it, not without her. Cotton candy shouldn't even exist anymore without her.

I look over Steven's shoulder. He's writing the game stats in the program, keeping track of each pitch, ball, and strike. Dad taught him how to fill in the scoresheet; they used to do it together. Now, Steven tackles it alone, asking David for help when he needs it.

During a break in the game as the teams switch sides,

David leans over toward Steven. "I'm going to buy some hot dogs. How many do you want, Steven?"

"Two," Steven says. "Just ketchup."

"Just ketchup, what?" I say to Steven.

"Just ketchup, please."

"Okay, got it." David stands up and carefully passes in front of Steven's legs, then mine, in the narrow row. "How about you, Sarah?"

I reach for my purse. "Sure, I'll take one."

"Your money's no good with me." He steps into the aisle. "Come on."

"Coke?"

I sigh and give in. "Yes, that's fine, thanks. Steven?"

"Sprite, no ice, please," Steven says.

"Can you carry all that?" I ask him.

"Yeah. They have drink carriers." He heads up the aisle steps and is back a few minutes later, laden with food. He hands me the drinks as he walks past me to get back to his seat. The hot dogs are all stacked on his arm against his chest. He gives Steven his two and passes one to me. From under his arm, he pulls out a slightly squished package of cotton candy.

"Here, Sarah. This is for you."

I stare at the familiar pink and blue cloud ensconced in plastic. He holds it out to me, but I don't take it. "Thank you, but I didn't ask for this."

"I know," he says, his hand still extended. "I just thought you might want one. You seem like someone who enjoys cotton candy."

"Well, thank you, but—"

"She does like it," Steven says as he grabs the plastic bag and puts it in my lap. "But it's too big for her. She needs someone to share it with. She used to always share it with my mom when we came to games. Maybe you can share it with her, David."

"Sure," David says, his gaze shifting toward the ground.

I pick up the cotton candy in my lap and move it from hand to hand. "That's fine. I mean sure, you can share it or whatever. Or maybe I'll just save it for later. Thanks."

"I'm sorry," David says, looking back up at me.

"Sorry? No. It's fine."

David nods and turns his attention back to the game. I take small bites of my hot dog and balance the cotton candy on my lap. At times, I look down at it, and all I can see is my mother's face, her lips tinted blue from the color of the cotton candy. Finally I tuck it into my purse. What will I do with it once I have it at home? I can't eat it, but throwing it away doesn't seem right either.

During the seventh-inning stretch, I go to the bathroom. I can't listen to "Take Me Out to the Ballgame." The lyrics, amplified through the stadium, follow me into the stall. I cover my ears and shut my eyes against the image of my mother, standing on her seat waving her hands in the air as she sings out into the crowd.

I wait well past the end of the song before leaving the refuge of the bathroom. There are still two long innings left.

"Everything okay?" David asks me when I return to my seat.

"Yeah. Long line."

Steven turns to me. "You missed the seventh-inning stretch. That was Mom's favorite part."

For an eight-year-old, Steven can be surprisingly observant at times. Usually when I don't want him to be. I don't respond to Steven, but I can feel David's eyes on me.

After the game, we follow the crowds leaving the stadium and walk back to the car. Traffic slows down as fans make a mass exodus from town and onto the freeway. I can hear Steven riffling through his program in the back seat.

"So, in the first inning there was one hit, one strikeout, one pop fly, another hit, and one groundout. Then the Astros had two hits, two strikeouts, one walk, and one groundout . . ."

David turns the music down. Steven summarizes all nine innings, reading the information he's written in his program. After he finishes, he puts his program away and turns back to his iPad.

I smile at David, thankful for his indulgence of Steven.

He smiles back before turning to the traffic in front of him. "I'm sorry," David says.

"For the traffic?" I ask.

"No. For all the memories. Of your mother. I didn't realize . . ."

"I didn't either. I hadn't really thought about it until I was there. But don't feel bad. It's fine." I add in a whisper, "Steven just has a big mouth."

"I'm sorry about the cotton candy too."

"It's okay. It's fine."

"You keep saying that it's fine, but is it?"

"It will be. I just—I'm sorry, I just don't want to talk about it."

"Okay." David increases the volume on the stereo. "I wouldn't mind if you wanted to take a nap, if you're tired. Don't feel like you have to stay awake or anything."

"Do I look that tired?"

"No, but in case you are."

"Okay. I think I will." I curl my legs up under me and push

the seat back a little. I close my eyes and try to think of nothing. Thinking of nothing is very difficult, but I force myself.

When I wake up, it's been more than an hour. Steven is still glued to the movie on his iPad. David is listening to a sports radio station. I ease my eyes open but stay in the reclined position.

"You want to stop or anything?" David says, turning to me.

"No, I'm okay. Thanks. That nap was just what I needed, I think."

"No problem."

Eventually, David pulls up into our driveway. He gets out and opens the door for Steven. Steven climbs out, holding his iPad and his program, now with bent and crumbling pages.

"What do you tell David?" I prompt him as David walks us to the front door.

"Thanks, David. I had a really good time. Can we go again?"

David laughs. "Sure, but the season's almost over. Playoff tickets are hard to get, but we can go again next year."

"How about opening day?" Steven asks.

"Steven!" I say, thinking of the cost of opening-day tickets. "No."

David laughs. "We'll see, Steven. We'll find a good game to go to."

"Okay. I have to go put this away now," he says, holding up his program. "I have a binder I keep all my programs in."

"I'm glad you had fun. Good night." David waves as Steven lets himself into the house.

"Thanks so much for everything," I say before I go inside too. "He had such a great time. It made his whole month, maybe even year."

"Good. I hope you had a great time too. I'm sorry if you didn't."

"I did. I just spent the day with two of the nicest guys. What more could a girl ask for?"

David jingles his keys in his hand. "Well, good night. I guess I'll see you Monday."

"Good night." I close the door behind me and lean back against it. It has been a good day. Steven enjoyed himself. He hasn't had such a good Saturday in a long time. I try to focus on that—and on how cute David looked in the Astros hat—instead of on the memories of Mom and the longing to have her with us again. Suddenly I remember the cotton candy hiding in my purse. I walk into the kitchen, take the package out, and put it in a cupboard that holds rarely-used baking supplies. I turn off the light in the kitchen and go upstairs.

Dad is asleep in his recliner. The scrambled eggs and bacon I made for him this morning are half eaten, and the peanut butter sandwich and fruit I left him for lunch are untouched. I'll clean it up tomorrow. Tonight, all I want is my bed.

CHAPTER EIGHT

"We're leaving in about an hour," I tell Steven when I find him in the living room at the computer. He's typing up box scores from last night, a newspaper in one hand and the other hand on the keyboard.

"Leaving to go where?" he asks.

"The festival at my school. Remember? I told you about the caramel apples."

"What else are they going to have?" he asks.

"Games and prizes—just, you know, festival stuff."

"What did you say were on the caramel apples?"

"Let's see, I saw some with a layer of drizzled chocolate. There were some with sprinkles, chocolate chips, mini M&Ms, candy—all kinds of things. They looked really good."

"Yum. I want one with sprinkles."

"Okay, so it starts in an hour." Steven nods and turns back to the computer. That gives me an hour to do homework. I sit at the kitchen table with my Spanish textbook.

I remember Mom's disappointment at the end of fifth grade when I told her I wanted to take French the next year. She lobbied for me to take Spanish, but I wanted to speak the language of my favorite artists: Claude Monet, Vincent van Gogh, Mary Cassatt. No amount of urging, bribery, or guilt-tripping from

Mom would change my mind. And now as I struggle through the conjugation of Spanish verbs, I concur with fifth-grade me. The French language has fewer verb tenses than Spanish, for one thing. Señora Dominguez seems really nice, but my brain isn't absorbing her lessons.

I shove my Spanish textbook closed and slide it across the kitchen table. I remember a book of Spanish verb tenses that Mom once flaunted to me as incentive. Maybe that'll help me with these conjugations.

As I walk into the office she shared with Dad, I'm hit with the stark differences between the two sides. His desk is strewn with old textbooks. A world map in muted colors collects dust on his wall, along with his bookshelves. Mom's side is dominated by a huge print of a Diego Rivera painting, which I've never liked but which definitely draws the eye. A trio of succulents sits on the corner of her desk. They're used to going without water for long periods, but they weren't designed for this kind of abandonment. I haven't looked at those succulents since before Mom died. My job is to keep a human child alive; I can't allow the guilt from those wrinkly, shriveled-up plants to penetrate the thin shield that's keeping me together, keeping me from completely falling apart.

I force my eyes away from the wilted succulents and search Mom's bookcase. It's obsessively organized. The top shelf is all books of Latin American history, followed by books of US and Latin American relations—subjects she taught at UTSA. The next two shelves are alphabetized fiction and poetry, starting with Allende and ending in Yeats. The fourth shelf is nonfiction, mostly biographies. I pull out a children's book about Diego Rivera that she gave me years ago. She must've found it abandoned in my room and rehoused it here.

I lower myself to the floor to more carefully read the spines of these books. There are at least half a dozen books about Spanish, Mexican, and Guatemalan artists. This was an argument that she restarted with me every few months. *Why don't you study Diego Rivera's techniques, his use of vibrant colors?* she would ask me. *Look at Rina Lazo's murals, at how they express a political and social consciousness*, she would say. But I don't like the bright colors that Diego Rivera used. I like the warm tones of Claude Monet and Mary Cassatt. I shove away the memories of these arguments, spot the Spanish verb book, and hurry out, closing the door behind me.

The book helps me with the Spanish homework, and I quickly read through the next physics chapter before Steven comes to stand in front of me, shoes tied, ready to go.

When we arrive at the high school, the festival is in full swing. On the blacktop, there are games with prizes, two bouncy houses, and a dunking booth where students can dunk teachers. Kids are scattered among the booths. PTA parents sell food in the cafeteria. Steven and I go inside for pizza and soda. He asks for the caramel apples, and I tell him we'll look for them after we've digested the pizza.

I buy some tickets for the games and go back outside with Steven. He speeds to the bouncy house.

"Steven!" a redheaded boy in a striped shirt shouts.

I recognize him from the bus stop, and Steven once told me his name, but I've forgotten. Steven runs toward him, and together they get in line for the bouncy house. I find a nearby bench and watch as Steven and his friend jump inside the bouncy house for the allotted five minutes. They quickly get back in line to go again. The friend's mom calls him after the second time, and Steven walks over to me, panting from all the jumping.

"What's your friend's name?" I ask Steven.

"That's Ryan. We were in chess club last year and we ride the bus together."

"You were in chess club?" I ask, realizing that when I was away in Austin, there was a lot I didn't know about his daily life.

"Yeah. It's going to start again in a few weeks. Can I do it again?"

"For sure. I think that sounds great." We walk toward a section of booths with various games. Steven stands in line to do a ring toss.

Near the adjacent booth, I notice a loose cluster of high school students, including David. He's talking to a girl with long brown hair. I've seen her before, walking with and sitting with Brad—who, mercifully, is nowhere in sight.

"David!" Steven says, leaving the ring toss line and going over to the other booth. "Hey, did you see the Astros last night?"

"Hey, Steven! That was a big win. Did you see the grand slam in the bottom of the eighth?" David gives him a warm smile and waves at me.

"Yeah, and in the first inning, the Astros had one strikeout, two hits, one groundout, and one pop fly. In the second inning, they had no strikeouts, one hit, two pop flies, and an out at second. And then in the third inning—"

The brown-haired girl snorts. "David, who is this little freak?"

"Shut up, Brittany," David says sharply.

I put a hand on Steven's shoulder and gently move Steven behind me. "He's a freaking genius, and on your smartest day, you're still dumb as shit compared to him."

"Mom says don't swear, Sarah," Steven says, but he doesn't hesitate to walk away with me.

David comes bounding behind us. "I am so sorry. I can't believe she said that." He taps Steven on the shoulder. "I'm really sorry she said that to you."

"Is she your friend?" Steven asks.

"Kind of, but I don't know her very well. I guess she's not very nice."

Steven frowns and shakes his head. "No. Not very nice."

"I'm really sorry," David says. I've never seen his brown eyes so subdued, so uncertain.

"You didn't do anything, David," Steven says.

"I know, but I still feel bad about how she treated you."

I squeeze Steven's shoulder. "Let's go, Steven."

David looks from Steven to me and back. "Hey, I'll show you which booth has the best popcorn, okay?"

"Yeah!" Steven says.

"Steven, I think we should go home."

"No, I want popcorn and we didn't get the apples yet."

I wish David would go away. I don't want him here right now, but he gives me a pleading look. I know he didn't do anything wrong, but I really just want to get Steven out of here.

David walks toward the entrance of the school. Steven follows him, so by default I do too. "So, this booth has the best popcorn, and I want you to meet the guys running it." David weaves through a crowd of elementary-aged kids in the hallway. We approach a large booth decorated in green and white, Richards High's colors. Five high school guys in football jerseys stand behind the booth. "Hey, Bobby," David says. "Can we get some of that popcorn for my friend Steven here?"

A tall dark-haired guy approaches us on his side of the booth. "Hey, David." He holds out his hand for a high-five/handshake combo.

"Bobby, this is Steven. He's one of your biggest fans, and this is Sarah."

Bobby nods at me and leans over the counter of the booth to Steven's eye level. "Hey, Steven. You're a friend of David's?"

Steven's eyes go wide. "Yeah. And you're my favorite player. I watch every game."

"Thanks, bud. That means a lot. Want some popcorn?" Bobby goes over to the popcorn machine stationed behind him. He fills a paper bag to the brim with popcorn and brings it over to Steven.

"Thanks, Bobby." Steven takes the bag of popcorn.

"And thank you, Steven, for coming by." Bobby calls two of the other players over to meet Steven. They talk for a minute, and the players all give Steven high-fives.

"Hey, can I get a few pics?" David asks, taking out his phone. Bobby and two other players come around in front of the booth and pose next to Steven, kneeling to fit in the frame. David takes four pictures. "I'll text them to you," he says to me.

"Thanks," I say as I watch Steven beaming, surrounded by these football players he idolizes.

David gives each guy a fist bump while Steven digs into his popcorn.

In my back pocket, my phone buzzes with the text. "Thanks, David. That was very nice."

"Sure. They love meeting fans. It makes their heads big."

Steven puts a handful of popcorn in his mouth. "I like these friends better than the other ones, David," he says.

"Me too, bud."

We stop to get caramel apples, and David walks Steven and me to my car. The apples are as delicious as I expected—maybe more so.

CHAPTER NINE

On Wednesday, right after Alexa and I finish on FaceTime, David finds me at the courtyard picnic tables. "Are you free on Saturday?" he asks, eyebrows raised in anticipation of my response.

I sigh. "David, I am free, but my life's too complicated right now."

"Too complicated for dinner?"

"Too complicated for anything." I look down at my half-eaten sandwich. "I'm sorry. You're so nice. But I can't do this to you."

"Do what? You're not doing anything to me."

"I just don't have any place for dating in my life right now. Steven is my priority."

"I understand," David says.

I'm not sure he does. He still looks hopeful. I shake my head. "It's just better this way, trust me."

"Better what way?"

"As friends."

"Friends can have dinner, right?"

I smile despite my resolve not to. "Is that all you think about? Food?"

"Come to dinner with me and you can find out. Just as friends."

I look away to squash a smile. "What time?"

"Six?" David cranes his neck to look at me. The wrinkles around his eyes are back. "Is six okay?"

"Yes, six is fine."

"Bring Steven if he wants to come."

This simple statement reaches the most tender piece of my heart. "I'll ask him."

I've asked Steven if he'd like to go to dinner with David and me and he's agreed, but when I go check on him on Saturday evening, he's immersed in reorganizing his baseball cards and doesn't want to be disturbed. He has piles scattered on the floor of his bedroom and is sitting in the middle of them, digging through boxes. He says he wants to eat at home, so I bring him a grilled ham-and-cheese sandwich and set the plate on his dresser.

"Are you sure you don't want to come?"

"Yeah. I can't leave right now. I have to stay here until I'm finished organizing these cards."

"Okay, but make sure to at least eat your dinner. I'm leaving it right here." I lean against the doorframe and watch as he sifts through the cards, quickly placing them in different stacks. I scan the room, guessing there are more than forty piles. I don't know how he's arranging them, but his hands do, and they work at a fast pace.

He'll be okay for a little while, I tell myself. I don't like leaving him at home, but sometimes I do for short periods—a few times a week when I have to run errands and he doesn't want to go along. Plus, of course, he gets home from school before me every day. I'll only be gone an hour or two, and I'll have my phone with me.

I bring Dad a plate and notice that his food from lunch is still on the tray table, untouched. He's lying on his stomach, his body sideways across the bed, his shoes still on his feet, hanging over the edge. His arms are spread out away from him. I watch his still form and wonder how long he's been like that. If he could just manage to get himself off this bed, I could be back at PFA with my friends and taking the classes I love.

He looks so different from the man I've called "Dad" all my life. Always clean-shaven, he kept his hair short and neatly combed. He even carried a little black comb in his pocket. Anytime we'd go somewhere, he'd comb his hair in front of the rearview mirror before starting up the car.

I wonder where that little comb is now. It surely hasn't been used in days. His greasy hair is longer than I've ever seen it, and his scraggly beard is growing wildly. This is not the man I used to take long bike rides with, the man who flew kites with me. This is an empty shell of a man—his body remains, but the spirit is entombed with my mom. He goes on living only because he has to, but there's no life left in him, and I wonder if there ever will be again.

I leave both plates and stumble out of the room. Tonight is not a night for tears. I've shed a lifetime of tears for the man my dad used to be. I've run through the gamut of emotions—pity, shame, sadness, anger—and the only feeling left is duty. That's what compels me to bring him meals every day, to wash his clothes and sheets and towels, to keep suggesting therapy. I go to my room to give some time to the one person I seem to always neglect—myself.

Getting ready for a first date. I haven't done it in a while and have almost forgotten the necessary rituals. My instinct is to throw my hair in a ponytail, but I resist. I comb my fingers through the curls and then push it all off my shoulders. I pick up a tube of lipstick that I haven't worn in months. Someone gave it to me for Christmas one year and I wear it rarely, only when I start feeling ungrateful for the gift. I take off the lid, examine the reddish tint, toss it back into the drawer. Inside is a small bottle of yellow perfume, also a gift from long ago. I think about misting some on my neck, but then I remember what the stuff smells like. Maybe I should change my white shirt, which has a tiny spot of butter from Steven's grilled ham-and-cheese. I throw the shirt to the floor and pull on a dark gray one.

The doorbell rings, and I slip on my sandals. As I open the door, a warm breeze pulls in the heavy scent of cologne. It isn't the strong type, but rather a rugged, woody smell that tickles my nose.

"Hi," I say. "You smell good."

He closes his eyes and grimaces. "I overdid it, didn't I? It's too much?"

"No. I like it. You'll smell good enough for the both of us."

David widens his smile and steps inside. "Is Steven coming?"

"No, he changed his mind. He got wrapped up with something."

"Can I say hi to him?"

I think about Dad passed out in bed. At least Steven's room is closer to the stairs. "Sure, come on up."

He follows me to Steven's open door.

"Hey, Steven. What are you working on there?" David asks.

Steven shuffles though the stack of cards he holds in his hand. "Just sorting my baseball cards."

"Can I take a look?" David walks over to Steven, careful not to step on the neat stacks, and crouches next to him. He watches Steven's fluid hands for a moment. Steven works quietly, placing cards into stacks and making a few new stacks. The number of stacks scattered around the room has multiplied since I was last in here. There's one big pile that seems to be a discard pile.

"Can I see a couple of them?" David asks, holding out his hand.

Steven gives him a handful and returns to his task. David studies one of the cards Steven has given him and scans the floor. He places a card down on one stack and looks at the next card. Steven pauses and looks at the card David has put down. Satisfied it's in the correct location, he continues his task. David puts down a few more cards, and Steven checks each one to make sure it's in an acceptable pile.

I watch in silence. There seems to be no logic to Steven's incessant stacking. But David works alongside him in quiet understanding. Whatever system or classification Steven is experimenting with, David has figured it out in mere moments. I just stare, admiration and shock competing for dominance in my head.

David lays down the last of the cards that Steven allotted him and looks up. "Sorry. You're probably ready to go."

I shake my head, words failing me. Dinner is the farthest thing from my mind.

David stands up from his crouched position. "Are you sure you don't want to come, Steven?"

Steven keeps stacking cards and doesn't look up. "No. I want to finish this tonight."

"Okay. Maybe we'll bring you back some dessert."

"Okay." Steven grabs another stack of cards from a nearby box.

"I've got my phone. Call me if you need anything," I tell him. Steven nods but doesn't look up.

David walks toward the door and turns around. "You've got a great collection here. Maybe someday I'll bring mine over and show you. I don't have as many, but I've got them all in two albums."

Steven's head shoots up. "You've got baseball cards too?"

"Oh, yeah. I don't have as many as you, though."

"Some of these are my dad's. He gave them to me because he doesn't want them anymore. Do you have any Roger Clemens? Or Cal Ripken? Or Barry Bonds?"

"I have an old Roger Clemens, I think."

"Do you have a rookie Nolan Ryan? My dad gave me a rookie Nolan Ryan, but I keep it in my drawer."

"Maybe next time you can show it to me."

"Okay." Steven lowers his head to look at the cards again. "Bye."

Once David and I are in his car, I ask, "How did you do that?"

"What?" David asks, backing out of the driveway.

"How did you figure out what he was doing?"

"I just looked at the stacks. He was organizing them according to career total batting averages. You know, two-eighty-twos all go in one stack, two-seventy-fives in another, and so on."

"And there are that many stacks?"

David laughs. "Yeah. Potentially, there could be over three hundred stacks. It just depends."

"And what about that big pile next to him?"

"Those were all pitchers. They don't have batting averages, so he was just putting them there." He shrugs. "I don't know. Maybe he's going to sort them later according to ERAs."

I want to penetrate his mind and figure out what he's thinking at the moment. Is he trying to impress me by edging close to Steven? Or is his kindness toward Steven, his enthusiasm for Steven's interests, actually genuine? "What's ERA?"

"Earned Run Average. You don't know anything about baseball, do you?"

"Actually, I know more than I want to know."

"Now you just have to learn to love it."

I laugh, which releases my knotted emotions. "I don't know if *that* will ever happen."

"Have you ever been to that Chinese restaurant down the street from here?"

I look down the road to where he's pointing. "No. I pass by it every day, but I've never been there."

"I heard it's good. Do you want to try it?"

"That's fine."

"I was going to take you guys to this amazing steak place downtown, but you probably don't want to go too far, right?"

"Is that okay?"

David pulls into the small parking lot. "Yeah, we can go to the steak place another day, when Steven wants to come."

"You're making it sound like I'm going to go out with you again."

"Oh, you'll go out with me again," he says with a grin as he opens the car door.

This would've sounded arrogant coming from anyone else, but not David. That word could never describe him. In fact, I wonder where his vast supply of kindness originates.

CHAPTER TEN

"Do you know how to tell if the food will be really good in a restaurant before you even taste it?" David asks when we're seated at our table.

"How?"

"The silverware doesn't match." He shows me a spoon with a skinny oval handle and a square-handled fork. "If they don't put much emphasis on appearance—matching silverware and plates—then their focus is on the food. When you go into a fancy restaurant where everything matches, then usually the food isn't very good."

"Really? I never noticed that."

"Stick with me," he says, winking. "I'll teach you all the secrets to finding the best food."

"So, you guarantee the food here will be good?"

"Yes. I guarantee it or your money back. Or, in this case, if you don't like it, then I'll have to take you somewhere else another day to make up for it."

I narrow my eyes. "That sounds like a trick."

"One of many."

I glance down at my purse and check to make sure my phone is set to chime with any incoming texts. I look through the menu, and we order our meals.

David watches me. A question dances in his eyes, and he seems to be thinking about how to phrase it. Personal questions come easily to him, but the answers don't come easily for me. So I beat him to it.

"So, is all your family here in San Antonio?" I am curious about his background, but I blurt out the question mostly to head off whatever he's intent on asking.

"Yeah. I was born in San Antonio, lived here all my life. All my cousins, tias, and tios live here in town. My grandparents came here from Mexico."

"Do you speak Spanish?"

He winces. "A little and really badly. My mom grew up speaking Spanish, but nobody spoke it at home when I was growing up. I learned a few words from my grandma, but just the basics, and a few bad ones from my grandpa."

I laugh. "That's okay. Nothing to be embarrassed about. My mom spoke a little Spanish too, but I also only know a few words."

He shrugs. "Sometimes I do feel bad about it. I guess it's just the older generation looking down on me, like I forgot my roots or something. I can't tell you how many times I get an older person shaking their finger at me because I don't speak Spanish."

"People judge us all the time for things they think we should be doing. You can't let it get to you. I've had my share of finger shaking, and I just ignore it now. Tell me about your family."

He smiles and leans in to take a sip from his water glass. "You really want to know about my family or you just want to not talk about yours?"

"Guilty. Tell me about them."

"Okay." He leans back in his chair. "My mom is a nurse, labor and delivery, and my dad sells insurance. Is that the kind of stuff you want to know?"

"Sure, why not? What else? Is your family really close?"

"Yeah, you know—dinner together every night, Mom checks in with me at bedtime."

"Every night?"

He looks sheepish but nods. "Every night. She just wants to make sure I've had a good day."

I smile, even as a shooting pain courses through me. The absence of my mother stings, and it's intensified by hearing about David's relationship with his mom. I feel guilty about that; I don't wish him ill. It's just the absence of my mother that hurts.

"I'm sorry." David reaches for my hand.

I bring both hands down into my lap. "No. Don't be. I'm fine."

The waiter brings our meals, quelling the awkwardness. I fill my mouth with steaming rice to avoid conversation. It's hot, and I immediately regret being hasty. I cool off my mouth with a long drink of water. We talk about lighter topics: how we each decided we want to be teachers, how we're excited for our COOP class. David is easy and fun to talk to once the topic of my family is off the table.

In the car on the way home, I feel seventeen. That's my actual age, but I've felt a lot older during the last six months. Right now, I'm almost the person I used to be—the one who lives for herself, who dates, who has friends and goes out on weekends.

David gives me a smile that stretches the length of his face. "So, can I hang out with you again?"

I want to say yes, though I shouldn't. Steven needs me, and as long as he does, I have to put him first, even if that means ignoring my own needs.

The thought pierces me with guilt. I love Steven and my dad and want to take care of them. I want to be there for them. I want to honor this responsibility left to me by my mom, who gave us all she had. But there is a part of me that wants something for myself.

David turns onto my street, and I'm hit by the familiarity of my surroundings, the recollection that I am the same Sarah from this morning.

David pulls up to the house, and—*Wait a minute.* I sit forward in my seat to clutch the dashboard. "Where's my car?"

"It was here when we left," David says.

I'm already across the lawn and sprinting to the house. "Steven!" I yell as I throw open the door.

"What?" he asks from upstairs.

I bolt up the stairs. "Where's my car?"

"I think Dad took it. He said he'd be right back."

"Steven!" I say, charging into his room. "Dad is never supposed to take my car!"

"Why?" Steven is still sorting his cards.

"Why didn't you call me?"

He shrugs and looks up. "He said he'd be right back."

"When did he leave?"

He looks at his phone. "Twenty-six minutes ago."

How did he get into the car anyway? My keys are in my purse, I'm sure of it. Ah, the extra set in the kitchen drawer. I've always kept a set there just in case. I turn around to go down the stairs just as David is coming up. "Is everything all right?" he asks.

"No. I have to find my dad. Steven, we'll be right back. Call me if Dad comes home. Steven!"

He looks up. "Okay, Sarah. I'll call you if he comes home."

"The second he comes home!"

"Okay, Sarah!"

I sprint down the stairs and hear David following me. At the front door I turn to face him. "Can you please drive me around? I have to find my dad."

"Of course. What's the matter?"

"My dad—he shouldn't be driving." I think of the series of empty Scotch bottles I've seen make their way into the recycling bin. "I think he's been drinking. Can you take me to the liquor store a few miles down?"

David drives in silence. He's probably thinking about my drunken father and pitying me.

I fiddle with my seatbelt, pulling it out and releasing it. I scan the streets, twisting my neck left and right as I search for my blue Toyota. My father hasn't driven since the bank repossessed his Lexus. Unfortunately, today there was a car accessible to him. I have to find him.

The lights of oncoming cars blind my teary eyes, and I shut them. Behind my closed lids, there is darkness and then an image of a car, out of control, careening toward a person, another car, a brick wall. The images flash in my mind in rapid succession, and I have to open my eyes to make them vanish. "The liquor store is after this light on your left."

David stops at the light and lets out a long, slow breath. "I'm sorry, Sarah."

I swipe away the two tears that roll down my face.

David proceeds through the light and pulls into the parking lot in front of the liquor store. I scan the parking lot and there it is—my blue Toyota. It's parked at the far end, by the curb.

I unbuckle my seatbelt and sit forward, reaching for the door before David has even fully come to a stop.

As I run toward my car, it inches forward into the curb. It jerks back and pauses for a moment before going in reverse.

I wave my arms and yell for him to stop. He doesn't see me, or ignores me, and inches forward in jerky movements. The car starts going in reverse again, and finally I reach the driver's side door.

He stops and looks at me with a blank face. I pound on the window with my fist. The window rolls down, and my father looks at me with a faint smile. A smile I haven't seen in a long time, one I almost can't remember at all.

"Sarah, hi. What are you doing here?"

"What are *you* doing here?" I scream.

The outburst startles him and he frowns. "Oh, Sarah. Sorry, I forgot to ask. Steven said you were on a date." His words are sincere—the words of a man who made a slight error, not one who endangered others' lives and his own.

"Get out of the car, Dad."

He opens the door and the car starts to roll backward. I scream and run after the car, which comes to a sudden halt just before it reaches the road. My father climbs out, an embarrassed look on his face, like he almost dropped a pitcher of water.

I'm beside him in an instant. He clutches a brown paper bag to his chest as if it's a baby. His hair is flat on the left side and sticking up on the right.

"Is this your date?" he asks in a friendly, casual voice, looking over my shoulder. David must be right behind me.

"Dad, I'll drive you home. Get in the car."

I open the back passenger door for him and he crawls into the back seat, his legs curled up in front of him, still clutching the bag to his chest. I slam the door with one swift motion.

David walks over to me, extending his hand. "Are you okay?" He brings his hand to my shoulder.

"I'm sorry about this. I'm going to take him home. You should probably get going."

"I can follow you back, make sure you get there okay."

I shake my head and avert my eyes. "No. Go home."

"Sarah, please. Let me help."

"No. Don't you see? This was a mistake. I never should've gone out with you tonight. I knew that. I knew that!"

"This is not your fault."

I shake my head. "No, and it's not yours either. But it is my problem, my life." Going out to dinner, dating, good-smelling guys—that's not my life. I can't have those things in my life. If I let my guard down for a minute, I could lose everything.

I open the driver's side door. "I can't do this. I'm sorry. I tried telling you that. Life is too complicated for me right now. This is all I can handle," I say, pointing to the car.

I close the car door, but David leans down to face me through the open window. "Don't shut me out. I want to help."

"I can't give you what you want."

"I'm not asking you to give me anything."

I shift into drive. "But you will, and I have no more to give. I already give everything I have."

He stands up and steps away from the car, and I pull away. There's no need to suppress the tears anymore. They stream down my face with no intention of letting up. I look in the rear-view mirror at David alone in the parking lot. His hands are in his pockets, and he watches me drive away. From the back seat, I hear snores.

CHAPTER ELEVEN

On Sunday morning, I bolt upright in bed as soon as I'm conscious. A sudden urgency to check the house pulls me from under the covers. I walk to Steven's room—he's still asleep, his lanky legs hanging over the side of the bed, his sheets discarded on the floor. As I pass my dad's room, his soft snoring allays my fears. He's home, in bed. Thoughts of the night before haunted me as I slept. What if he'd crashed my car, hit someone, killed someone? I imagined all the ramifications—my father arrested, imprisoned, or possibly dead. And what those consequences would mean for Steven are equally frightening.

Back in my own room, I pull my bedcover off the bed and drag it to my window seat, where I tuck it around my legs and stare out the window. I should probably get up and start my mile-high to-do list. I have to work on my Etsy projects, there is nothing but cereal to eat right now, and I have a mountain of homework to tackle. But I don't move; I need this moment to just sit here and think about none of those things.

Robert is outside, taking his collie for a walk. He's wearing a shirt this morning, but it'll probably be pulled off when he picks up his weed-whacker later in the day. I glance down at my car, parked askew in the driveway where I left it last night in my hurry to get Dad back in the house.

It was foolish of me to go out. To leave Steven, my father, the car. My mind flashes back to David's eyes, making me feel like I was more than just Steven's sister, more than just Paul Mosley's daughter. I was a girl who laughed and flirted and enjoyed spending time with a guy. I liked the scent of his cologne; it made me feel like there were possibilities. Real possibilities that didn't make me choose between being loved and abandoning my family—that would let me fulfill my responsibilities without sacrificing myself entirely.

For one night, I gave myself a reprieve from my duties. For a brief moment, I tasted of the luxury of being just a girl desired by somebody.

But this morning, as dawn sheds light on my life, I know better. There isn't enough of me to give Steven the stability he requires, to manage my dad's spiraling, *and* to allow myself the indulgence of being wanted the way David wants me. He wants me just for myself—the kind of want that has no need, unlike the demands that keep me at home.

If I give in to the desire to be looked at, to be touched, to be wanted by a guy, by David, then it will distract me from where I'm needed the most.

Monday morning. For the average person, it's a day to be dreaded—the end of the weekend's fun and relaxation. For me, who had an exhausting weekend, Monday is just a continuation of the bleakness.

On my way to physics, David catches up to me. "Hey, Sarah. I was thinking about you all weekend. How is everything at home?"

I see the kindness in the creases around his eyes. "I'm sorry about Saturday."

"You don't need to be sorry about anything," he says.

"But I am. It's not fair to you. I knew that going into it, and I shouldn't have let it get that far."

"It didn't get very far."

"One date is too far for me right now. You understand that, right?"

He shakes his head. "I understand that you're under a lot of stress and you're dealing with some heavy things, but does that mean you have to put your whole life on hold?"

I understand where he's coming from. But my life *is* on hold, whether that's fair or not. Dad is not going to start paying bills and buying groceries and doing laundry if I get distracted and let something slip. Steven is not going to turn from an eight-year-old into a self-sufficient teenager overnight. I can't prioritize them if I'm prioritizing a relationship. And I can't give a relationship the attention it deserves if I have to drop everything for my family at a moment's notice.

Right now, my focus has to be Steven; that's all I can commit to. Feelings for David, the desire to let him past that wall I've erected, have to be squelched.

"Let's not keep rehashing it. I need to ask you for something."

"Anything."

"Please don't tell anybody." I wasn't expecting my emotions to permeate the conversation, and I clear my throat to hold them back. Bursting into tears is no way to start a Monday. "I just don't want anyone here to know."

"I wouldn't tell anyone." David places his hand lightly on my elbow. My stiff muscles relax at his touch, and my entire body calms itself.

"Okay," I say, nodding. "Well, thank you. I knew I could trust you."

"You can always trust me," he says, dropping his hand into his pocket. "I told Steven I would bring my baseball cards over for him to see. Can I come by sometime this week?"

I know the kind boy standing in front of me will carefully guard my painful secret. But there's a decent chance of Saturday night replicating itself, so I don't feel up to letting him come over. "Maybe in a few weeks? I just need some time right now."

He nods as we walk into class. "I'm here if you need me. Always."

"Thank you." I take a seat and rummage through my backpack for my notebook. The busier I make myself, the less I'll think about him. Or so I hope. But images of his smile stay in my thoughts, interspersed with memories of the frantic search for my dad. Both cannot coexist in my life. As long as my dad's drinking poses a danger to himself and others—especially Steven—there can be no smiles from charming boys.

In COOP, Ms. Mesa tells us which elementary class each of us will do a lesson plan for and the date we'll present that lesson. David will go first, leading a fourth-grade gym class at the end of the month. I've been assigned to fourth-grade art on the second Friday in November. Makaila turns to me after Ms. Mesa tells her she's got third-grade science. "I'm so glad I don't have to teach first graders. What kind of science do you teach first graders? Older kids, I can work with. What do you think you'll plan your art lesson on?"

"Something with drawing, I think. That's pretty accessible—you don't need a lot of special tools for it or have to spend more than one class period making something." I stand up as the bell rings for the end of the period.

"That's a good point. We'll have to cram whatever we're doing into a thirty-minute class session. Hey, you want to sit with my friends and me at lunch?"

I guess it can't hurt to eat lunch with someone in person for a change. "Sure. That sounds good." I text Alexa that I'm going to eat with a friend from class, and she sends back a smiling emoji.

ALEXA: Yay, friends!

As I follow Makaila out the door, I glance in David's direction. He smiles and gives me a little wave. I smile and wave back.

After lunch, I have my advanced art class. There are only ten students, and it's led by Ms. Escamilla, a five-foot-two Latina with a large voice who wears her hair in a short bob with bangs that cover her eyebrows. Her age could be anywhere from early thirties to late forties; it's hard to tell.

So far, we've mostly done small projects, but now Ms. Escamilla is telling us about a project due in December, at the end of the semester.

"You'll pick a theme for your project and write up a proposal. Proposals are due in two weeks. Your options for a theme are pretty much open. It can be a period of history or a country, an art movement, or even one particular artist. You will create at least eight original pieces based on this theme. They could be all one medium or mixed media. The details are up to you. At the end of the semester we'll have a showcase for your pieces. You'll each display your work however you want and give a five-to-ten-minute speech introducing your project. You are basically putting on an art show."

She goes on to show a PowerPoint presentation of past student art shows: images incorporating or inspired by nineties grunge album covers, historical events, van Gogh paintings, watercolor ocean landscapes, pencil drawings of the life cycle of a frog. She was not kidding when she said themes can be anything.

I spend the rest of the day trying to figure out what my theme could possibly be. It's refreshing to think about something other than what I'm making for dinner—and to focus on art other than drawings of families I don't even know.

CHAPTER TWELVE

When I walk into the house on Friday after school, I hear whistling coming from upstairs. There hasn't been whistling in the house in a long time.

I take the steps two at a time and come right up to a face I almost don't recognize. There's no scraggly beard—only a smooth, clear face. "You shaved!" I blurt out.

"It was time, Sarah. Time to clean up, time to go on."

My chest tightens as I look at my dad. This is the man I looked up to for most of my life. He pushed me on the swing in the backyard until my toes touched the leaves of the old oak tree. He taught me how to ride a bicycle on the sidewalk in front of the house. I thought I'd lost him.

I watch him for a moment before I say anything, wanting to believe this kind of shift is possible and actually happening. But there have been so many moments in the past few months when I thought there was a chance he'd come back. There was the day in July when he packed up the car and insisted we go fishing in Corpus Christi. We had a fun time together until he caught a fish, which reminded him of the day Mom caught her first fish on the same pier. He sobbed for an hour on the pier, earning stares from everyone there. Each time I've glimpsed his old self, it's been like that—short-lived, and often ending disastrously. I wonder about today. How long will it last before he disintegrates?

He closes the gap between us, pulling me into an embrace. Teddy bear hugs, he used to call them. I expect him to start weeping, but he doesn't. I rest my head on his shoulder and breathe him in. There's no stench of alcohol, only soap. His hair is still wet and smells of lavender—the shampoo Mom always used. I can feel strength in his shoulders, in his embrace. My daddy is back—the one who made *me* dinner, gave *me* counsel, took care of *me*.

He releases me from the hug. "I defrosted some chicken for dinner. I thought I'd marinate it for an hour and then we could grill it."

He speaks like it's just an ordinary day—making dinner plans like he hasn't just woken up from a self-induced coma. It feels strange, and I'm not sure how to react.

I trail him to the kitchen, where he begins rifling through the cupboard, pulling out random items that he places on the counter. He hasn't cooked a meal in months, and yet he acts as if it's something he still does every day.

He used to cook before—they both did. They took cooking classes together: Italian, Mexican, Indian. And they worked in tandem most nights preparing delicious meals. It was something they enjoyed doing jointly. It wasn't just dinner. For them, it was an activity that brought them closer. She would break the eggs, and he would whisk. She minced and chopped while he sautéed. I would set the table—always their best china. I loved dinners at home and was always willing to try new dishes. Steven would usually oblige as well, although if the meal was something especially unusual, there would always be noodles or potatoes to appease him.

I watch as Dad tenderizes the chicken. It must be hard for him, cooking without her.

"Can I help?" I ask.

He looks up at me and stares for a minute. "Sure. Do we have any lemons?"

"We do." I walk over to the refrigerator and bring one to him.

After he cuts and squeezes it, I take the remnants over to the garbage can. Next to the can is a bottle of Scotch. I wonder if he meant to put it inside. When he's not looking, I dump it in on top of the lemon husks. "Do you want me to throw some potatoes in the oven? We could have baked potatoes."

"No, she doesn't—" He stops.

"Right." Why did I say that? How could I have forgotten?

He shakes his head and turns back to pound on the chicken. "No. It's fine. Baked potatoes."

"I'd better go check on Steven," I say, walking out of the kitchen.

She doesn't like baked potatoes. She never did. Too plain. *You don't even do anything to them*, she would say. She firmly believed potatoes should be generously seasoned. But I make baked potatoes often now because they're easy. Steven likes them—he never complains about any type of potato.

Steven is in his room going through the newspaper. I knock on his open door. "Dad seems to be feeling better today. He's up and about. You might not even recognize him. He shaved his beard."

"Is he coming to the game tonight?"

I had forgotten all about the football game. I'm tempted to tell Steven we should stay home, but that would send him into an immediate tantrum. "I don't know if he'll want to go."

"I'll ask him," Steven says as he runs down the stairs.

When I return to the kitchen, Steven has the newspaper in hand and is reading Dad the baseball scores. Dad stirs the marinade and nods at intervals. There are three potatoes wrapped in foil on the counter.

A little over an hour later, the chicken has been grilled and lies in a Tupperware container in the middle of the table next to the foil-wrapped baked potatoes and some grilled corn on the cob. Mom's china hasn't been touched since the funeral; we use Corelle plates now. Dad didn't say anything about the way I set the table—it's nothing compared to how I used to do it when Mom was alive. I always wanted to impress her, taking the time to make sure each utensil was placed properly and carefully. Mom's compliments meant so much, even though they were bestowed in abundance.

Those days are in the past now. Minute details like that don't matter anymore. In fact, trying to recreate those days with proper table settings would seem blasphemous now. She isn't here to enjoy it, so it shouldn't be done.

Dad keeps his eyes on the table. His hands alternate between being folded in front of him and lying in his lap. I wait for him to start eating, but his nervous movements only increase. Finally, Steven stabs a baked potato. Dad and I follow his lead.

I remember the last time I saw Dad sit at the table to eat. I was home for winter break. He and Mom made rack of lamb, those little red potatoes, and sourdough rolls from scratch. *Beautiful* is what Mom called those potatoes. They were roasted to a golden hue, covered in butter, and drizzled with rosemary and parsley—such a vast difference from the plain potatoes that sit before us today.

The memory is so vivid. Dad talked about training for the San Antonio marathon and wanted to know who would enter it with him. He tried convincing Mom and me, but neither of us wanted to. He also surprised Mom by telling her he'd signed them up for Latin dancing lessons. Mom was so excited that she beamed for the rest of the night. I can still picture how she looked then: bright eyes, wide smile, and perked-up nose. It's my favorite way to remember her.

It feels so strange to be sitting here now—the three of us. For months, it's only been Steven and me eating at the table. Dad, when he eats, does so at the tray table I set up in his room. Sitting at this table for dinner will never be happy for him again. Steven and I are not enough for him. Today I'm more aware of that than ever, even more than when he was in a pit of grief. I can never bring Mom back, and the fact that Steven and I sit with him only makes her absence more apparent.

Steven convinces Dad to go to the football game. I'm still going too, worried that the man of the last six months will reemerge before halftime.

When we get to the high school, David is already sitting in our usual seats. His presence beside us at games has become customary, a fact that I'm still not entirely comfortable with. I wish he wasn't here today to be a witness to Dad's shaky attempt at sobriety.

He stands up as we approach. Steven is ahead of Dad and me, and he claims the seat next to David.

"Look, David. My dad's here. He woke up and can do stuff now."

David extends his hand. "Hi, Mr. Mosley. It's good to see you again."

Dad studies him as they shake hands. "I'm sorry. We've met before? I just can't place it. Forgive me."

"This is David Garza," I say flatly. "He's in two of my classes."

Dad gives David a businessman's smile. "I'm Paul Mosley. It's a pleasure, David."

We all sit. Steven's gaze is fixed on the field, the numbers rattling off in his brain, his lips moving softly in whispered recitation. I study Dad's face. His jaw is relaxed, his eyes calm. He sits forward in his seat with both elbows on his knees, his hands clasped together.

"So, David," he says. "You're a junior too?"

"Yes, sir."

"Have you decided where you're applying to college next year?"

"Dad, leave him alone," I interject.

David gives a small, polite laugh. "UTSA. I want to stay close to home, so I can do volunteer coaching in the community—get some experience so I can eventually get a job at one of the high schools, coaching basketball."

"I love San Antonio." Dad closes his eyes in contemplation. "We've been here now almost twenty years. We moved here right out of grad school in Boston when I got my position at UTSA."

"You work at UTSA?" David asks.

"Used to. I'm retired now, but I was a professor in the history department. I knew some professors in the kinesiology department. I can give you the names of the good ones, and the ones to stay away from."

"Dad, he hasn't even applied yet. Who knows, by the time

he even starts taking classes in the major, some of those professors might've *retired*," I say, holding up air quotes for the last word.

Dad clears his throat and looks out toward the field, silent.

"Sure, you can give me those names," David says.

Dad answers him without looking at him. "No problem. I'll write them down or something."

Richards scores a touchdown, and the crowd stands up. Steven announces the score and waits to hear the length of the touchdown.

"Twenty-eight-yard pass for a touchdown," the announcer says.

"Twenty-eight yards," Steven echoes. "That's good, right, Dad?"

"Pretty good." He slides his hands into his pockets and doesn't sit down when the rest of the crowd does. "Excuse me, I'm going to go to the bathroom. I'll be right back."

I let my dad squeeze past my legs and watch him walk away. I don't want him out of my sight for even a minute.

David taps my shoulder. "Are you okay?"

I turn to him and unclench my tight shoulders. "I don't know."

"Your dad's really nice," David says.

"Well, you've got him on a good night. Lucky you."

A few minutes later, Dad comes back, chewing gum, and takes his place. "What'd I miss?"

"Number forty-two is in now," Steven says. "His name is Marcus Rodriguez."

"You having fun, Steven?" Dad asks.

"Yeah, Dad. Richards has seven points now. Last game they scored twenty-four and the game before that was seventeen."

"That's good you can remember all that," Dad says. "So, David. What's your favorite sport?"

"It's hard to pick, but I'd have to say basketball. That's what I play and what I want to coach."

"Ah, so do you play for Richards?"

"Yes, sir. I play varsity."

"Well, we'll have to come see you play when the season starts. Steven, you want to watch David play basketball?"

"Sure," Steven says, not taking his eyes off the field. "And maybe next time you can come to the Astros game with us."

"The Astros game?" Dad asks, looking from me to David.

"Yeah, David took me and Sarah when the Astros beat the Mariners eight to two."

"Sarah, why didn't you tell me you and Steven went with David to an Astros game?"

"Whatever, Dad. I'm sure I mentioned it. You just forget everything."

Dad looks uneasily from me to David again. "She's right. I seem to forget a lot of things lately."

David forces a smile and turns to the field, where the marching band is assembling for the halftime performance.

After halftime, Dad excuses himself to go to the bathroom again while David is quizzing Steven about player stats. Ten minutes pass, and Dad still hasn't returned. It can't take that long to go to the bathroom. I keep turning my head to see if he's coming, but there's no sign of him. I sit on my hands and bounce my knees to keep from tearing away from my seat to go find him.

David is looking at me. "Do you want me to go check the restroom to see if he's okay?"

I look away from his compassionate eyes. He wants to help me, but I don't want him to see me this way, to see what my dad has become, to witness this humiliating time in my life. But he is here, and as awkward as I feel about this, I nod. "That would be great."

David jumps to his feet, but just as he's about to squeeze past Steven, he freezes. "Oh, hey, here he comes now."

I turn—and he's right, Dad is walking toward us. He rubs his hands together before reaching out for a railing to hold on to. David sits back down; I can tell he's trying not to stare, but his head keeps turning in Dad's direction.

Dad takes the bleacher steps slowly, watching his feet. When he's only a few rows behind us, his footing wavers and he grabs on to the shoulder of a woman seated at the end of a bleacher.

"Sorry, ma'am," he says with a smile as he uses her shoulder for support to make it to the next step.

I stand up and grab his arm to usher him into the row. "Sit down," I say.

He sits. "Not as young as I used to be," he says to David. "Got a little winded there. What'd I miss?" He runs his hands up and down his legs.

"Richards fumbled the ball," Steven says, oblivious to Dad's odd behavior.

There's a time-out now. Using Steven's head to help himself up, Dad stands. "Boo! Lousy call," he shouts at the field.

I grab his arm and pull him down.

"Boy, it feels good to be back out here. I can't believe I missed some of the games this season." He turns to Steven. "Isn't this great? Don't you love being out here?"

"Yeah, Dad."

He pats Steven on the shoulder. "Let's start the wave. Should we start the wave?"

"Stop it." I grab his wrist. "Let's just watch the game."

"I am watching the game. We're having fun."

"I think it's time to go," I say.

"But Richards has the ball," says Steven. "What if they score a touchdown?"

"I'm sorry, but I think we should go."

Steven stomps his feet and the woman in front of us turns around.

I dig into my purse, grasping for my keys as I stand up. "Come on, Steven."

"No!" he yells. "The game's not over."

"I know, but we have to go." I reach for his arm. "Dad's not well. We have to take him home."

"Well, you take him home and then come pick me up when the game's done."

"I'm fine, Sarah," Dad cuts in. "Stop ruining everything."

I swallow hard and avoid looking at David.

"Let's take Dad to the car, and then we'll talk about it." It's all I can think to say to get Steven to move. Out by the car, I will just have to tell him no. He'll scream and cry, but at least it won't be in front of all these people.

Steven stands up and I pull Dad to his feet. "Bye, David. We have to go," I say over my shoulder.

David is right behind me. I put my arm around my dad to help balance him. He's still mumbling something, but he doesn't put up much resistance as we hustle him along.

At the car, I open the door, and David helps me ease my dad into the back seat, where he lies down and presses his face against the warm leather interior. I slam the door shut, but the jolt doesn't rouse him.

Steven turns on his heel as soon as the door is closed. "Come on. Let's go back."

"Steven, wait." I take a step toward him. "We can't just leave Dad in the car. We're going to have to go home."

"Let me follow you home so I can help you bring him inside," David says.

"No, we'll be fine. Thanks for all you've done."

Steven walks over and stands right in front of me, pulling himself up on his toes to face me. "No! The game's not over. I don't want to go."

"Steven," I say, placing a calming hand on his shoulder.

He shrugs it off. "No!"

"I can stay with Steven until the game is over and then bring him home," David offers.

Gentle words from a gentle boy. I can't ask any more of him. Not tonight. "No, we'd better just go."

"But, Sarah. Why not?" Steven asks.

"It's just better this way."

Steven forms his hands into fists and slams them against his legs. "That doesn't even make any sense!"

I look at David, who stands with his hands deep in his pockets but says nothing more. I'm keenly aware of how uncomfortable this situation must be for him. "Okay," I say to him finally. "Are you sure you don't mind?"

"I don't mind at all. But are you sure you're okay on your own?"

I nod. "Yeah. I'm used to this."

Frown lines appear around his lips. "Okay, well, don't worry about us. We'll be fine; we'll be having a good time."

"Thank you. So much. You've done a lot for me tonight."

He reaches out to squeeze my hand. His hand is warm and strong. "I'll see you in a little while."

The crowd in the background cheers, and Steven turns

his head toward the field. "Come on, David. Let's go. What if Richards scored and we missed it?"

David turns around and jogs to catch up with Steven, who is sprinting across the parking lot.

As I drive home, I think I know what triggered Dad's unraveling. It probably started with the baked potatoes. And then there was the talk of UTSA, classes, professors—all those things from his past that only existed when she did. Thinking about them now had probably depressed him, reminded him of what he doesn't have anymore.

CHAPTER THIRTEEN

Dad's head is nodding and his eyes are fighting hard to close, but somehow I summon the strength to drag him inside. He musters enough energy to get up the stairs, with me spotting him, and finally collapses facedown on the bed. I roll him onto his side—I've heard stories from friends at PFA about drunk people choking on their own vomit. I don't know if Dad is drunk enough for that to happen, but I don't want to find out.

I shut his door behind me and lean against the wall next to it, still breathing hard. After a minute I trudge back downstairs to wait for David and Steven.

I lie down on the couch and adjust the blinds so I can see when they drive up. Closing my eyes for a moment, I dissect in my mind the events of the evening. If this doesn't chase David away, nothing will. Why is he still hanging around? What is he waiting for?

Me. He is waiting for me. But there isn't anything left of me to give. I have to make that clear to David, even though I already tried.

A pair of headlights flashes through the window, and I get off the couch and walk to the door.

Steven rushes in. "Look, Sarah. David bought me a new Richards High sweatshirt that I can wear to the games when it starts to get cold." He turns toward the stairs.

"Wait. What do you say to David?"

"Thanks!" He goes bouncing up the stairs to his room. "I've got to do the stats."

"Do the stats?" David asks, closing the front door behind him.

"Yeah. He likes to write down the scores and touchdowns for each Richards game. He keeps it in a notebook."

"Wow. That's impressive."

"Thanks for buying him that sweatshirt. You didn't have to do that."

"Am I in trouble?" he asks, hands clasped contritely behind his back.

"You couldn't be in trouble for anything tonight. Thanks for all you did to help."

"I imagine you're pretty stressed."

I shrug, part of me instinctively wanting to minimize it and part of me wanting to scream, *I'm beyond stressed*. "I'm embarrassed to say that it's an almost daily occurrence."

"Sorry."

I don't want him to leave, but it's been a long night, and I'm not sure what else to say to him. I already apologized a handful of times and thanked him excessively. Gratitude for his kindness extends from every cell in my body, but how else can I express that to him?

"We stopped for ice cream," David says, holding out a small paper bag he pulls from behind his back. "I bet you could use some."

I take the bag. "Thank you. You didn't have to do that."

"I know, but I wanted to. I'd do more, if you'd let me." He takes a step toward me.

"Do you want to sit down?" I ask, gesturing toward the couch with my head.

David follows me into the living room and sits next to me. "Steven said chocolate chip cookie dough is your favorite."

I lift the small cup of ice cream out of the bag and dig into it with a plastic spoon. "Mmm. It is."

"How old were you in this picture?" he asks, pointing to a framed photo of me hanging on the wall next to a framed photo of Steven.

"That was freshman year, a school picture."

"Wow, your hair looks so straight. It's so different."

"Yeah, I used to straighten it." Starting when I was eleven, I would flatten my curls after every shower with the help of a hair dryer, a large round brush, and a very hot flat-iron.

He looks between me and the picture. I wonder if he likes my hair better in that picture.

"I've just let it go curly lately," I add. "It's way easier."

"I really like it curly," he says. "It's really pretty."

It's definitely time to change the subject. I swallow a bite of ice cream, the coldness cooling my flushing face and soothing my tired throat on its way down. "I know I've said it a dozen times, but thank you for being there for Steven tonight."

"Anytime. How's your dad?"

I move around the remains of my ice cream with the plastic spoon. "I don't know. The same, really."

He leans forward, resting his elbows against his knees. "You can call me anytime you need me. I'll be here in a flash. You shouldn't have to go through this alone."

"Thanks, but you really don't—"

"No, Sarah. Stop." He reaches out for my hand. His long, warm fingers stroke my palm, taking away the lingering effects of the cold ice cream I was holding. "I am your friend. That's all—I know. But this is what friends do. They help each other. So, please promise me that you'll call me when you need me."

"I appreciate that, but I can't promise anything. I'm just trying to get through this the best I can."

"You're doing great. Better than I think anyone else could do." He pulls himself up to his feet. "I should go."

I stand up and follow him to the door.

"Take care of yourself. Tell Steven I said goodbye."

"Good night. Thank you for everything. I'm lucky to have you as a friend."

"Para servirle."

"What?"

He pulls out the smile that makes the corners of his eyes wrinkle. "That's one of the only phrases I know in Spanish. It means 'here to serve you.' My abuelita used to always say it instead of 'you're welcome.'"

His words soothe that part of me that feels so hopeless on nights like these. "Gracias. That's one of the only things *I* know in Spanish."

"Bye, Sarah."

I stand on the front stoop watching him as he backs his car out and drives away. One day, maybe. Not now, but maybe one day, I want him to hold my hand again like he did tonight. I want him to wrap his arms around me and run his fingers through my hair.

I go into the kitchen to throw away the empty ice cream container. The bottle of Scotch I placed in the garbage can isn't there. I start rummaging through the garbage can, hoping it's just buried at the bottom, but no. It isn't under the sink either. After a quick search of the kitchen and living room, I check the downstairs bathroom. There, next to the toilet on the floor, stands an empty bottle. And behind it is another one. Small objects, but with the power to destroy. They destroyed the small measure of happiness that existed for us today.

I grab each bottle by the neck and stomp into the garage. The green recycling tub is next to the door, but it is too good for these bottles. I hurl them against the garage wall on the far side where Dad's bicycle hangs, unused for months. They crash in quick succession, pieces of glass spraying onto the ground. The bicycle must not have been properly mounted, because it falls to the floor, knocking Steven's and my bicycles down like dominoes.

CHAPTER FOURTEEN

I wake to the sound of my phone ringing in my purse. I pull myself out of bed and look at the clock. Two in the morning. Who is calling me? I trip over my shoes in the darkness as I walk toward the ringing phone and answer it without looking at the caller ID.

"It's two o'clock in the morning!" Wanda's shrill voice announces, as if I haven't noticed.

"Wanda, why are you calling me?"

"Look out your window."

I slump onto the window seat, rub my eyes to clear my vision, and pull up the blinds. In the dim light of the streetlamp, I can see my dad, barefoot and in his pajamas. He holds a weed-whacker and is trimming the foot-high weeds near our drive-way, right outside Wanda's window. He stops and starts the trimmer several times, hacking at the already shredded weeds.

"Sorry, Wanda," I say into the phone. "I'll go get him."

"Next time, I call the police!" The slam of Wanda's land-line phone on its cradle ricochets against my ear. I throw my phone in the general direction of my purse before I sprint down the stairs and outside.

He doesn't see me or hear me when I call him. I walk up to him and grab for the weed-whacker. That startles him, and he lets go of it, letting it fall to the ground by our feet.

"Hi, Sarah. I'm sorry I let these weeds get out of hand. I'll finish up here and then dig up the backyard for our garden. I can't believe we're getting such a late start this year."

"No, you can't do this. It's the middle of the night. Wanda's threatening to call the police."

He looks over at Wanda's house and frowns. "She's so unreasonable."

"No, Dad, *you're* unreasonable. It's dark; you can't even see what you're doing. This is no time to do yardwork."

"I can see just fine," he says, bending to pick up the weed-whacker. He's about to turn it on again, but I snatch it from his hands.

"No. Let's go inside."

He deflates a bit. "I'm sorry, Sarah. I'm just trying to help. I haven't been pulling my weight around here."

"Now is not the time. It's time to sleep."

He follows me to the garage, and I set the weed-whacker on the ground before closing the garage door. We walk quietly into the house and up the stairs. There isn't anything more to say to him. I hear him close his door behind me as I continue to my room. My bedcover is on the floor and I pick it up, pulling it over my head as I lie down. Sleep doesn't come easily.

Several hours later, I wake up to the rays of a Saturday morning beaming through the blinds I left open last night. I stare up at the ceiling, not wanting to get out of bed. What purpose does it serve? I don't have school today. Steven and Dad are probably both sleeping in. There's housework to do, but who would even notice if the bathroom floors weren't cleaned or the carpet not vacuumed? Steven and Dad don't pay much attention to any of that.

I indulge myself in an hour of lying in bed with nothing to do but let my mind wander and my tired body rest. David is at the forefront of my thoughts. He's been so kind. So many reasons to be thankful to him, grateful for him; so many reasons to let him take that next step I know he wants to take. It's the same step *I* want to take.

Maybe it's not as unrealistic as I've convinced myself it is. Maybe being with him wouldn't have to get in the way of taking care of Steven and Dad. He would never expect me to neglect my family for his sake. But how could I ask him to put up with canceled or shortened plans, disruptions that range from annoying to dangerous? No one wants to date a person who can't ever be fully present or fully relaxed.

The ongoing war in my mind still hasn't reached a resolution. Doubts and equally compelling urges continue to battle.

I hear Steven walking around in his room and decide it's time to start the day.

After breakfast I spend two hours working on my Etsy portraits in my room while Steven works on a new project at the computer. When I take a break to check on him, he's immersed in the sports section of the newspaper, going over football scores.

"After you're done, why don't we go for a walk?" I ask him.

"I don't want to."

I'm tempted to let it go, leave him alone to his preferred activities, but he needs some time away from stats and numbers. Mom wouldn't want to see him stuck to a screen as much as I'm letting him get away with. She would insist on him getting some exercise and Vitamin D. "Come on. If you go on a walk with me, I'll let you stay up thirty minutes later."

"Fine." Steven goes to put his shoes on and meets me on the front step.

The weather has cooled to the low eighties, the Texas version of fall. We walk down to the neighborhood park where Mom used to take Steven when he was little. It's a small park used mostly by toddlers and young kids. He's definitely outgrown it. But I don't even know where else I could take him. I don't know where kids his age hang out. By the time I was eight, I was already spending most of my free time drawing, unless I was at a friend's house.

Steven stops for a minute just outside the gate leading to the park. "This is Mom's favorite tree in the neighborhood," he says. "Mom loves coming here in November when all the leaves turn yellow. She says it reminds her of Boston in the fall. She says this tree is the only thing that feels like fall around here."

I look up at the tall oak tree that provides shade for nearly all of the small park. "Yeah, I remember."

"Can we come back next month when the leaves turn yellow?"

"Of course."

Five blocks from home, a rain shower begins with no warning. I tilt my head back and look up into the sky. The raindrops blur my vision, so I close my eyes and let the water pour freely down my face. It's a freeing moment when nothing bothers me.

"Hurry, Sarah. We're getting all wet." Steven starts running, his hands covering his hair.

I run to catch up, my hands outstretched. There is nothing to do about the rain but to enjoy it—to let the eager drops soak every inch of my body. There are too many things in the world that bother me, worry me, make me afraid. Rain is not going to be one of them.

I catch up with Steven and grab him from behind. "Wait."

"No, Sarah. It's raining."

"We're already wet. Just enjoy it." I take his hand. Steven lets me, but he starts running again. I run beside him.

"Can't you imagine this is something Mom would do?" I say. "Let the rain fall on her, enjoy the moment?"

"I don't know."

"When I was little Mom used to let me jump in puddles. Don't you love to jump in puddles, Steven?"

"No, my shoes get wet."

I laugh. "Come on. Let's find a puddle."

We locate a promising puddle in front of Ms. Maldonado's house. I can remember taking walks with Mom before Steven was born. I would jump in puddles of rainwater, and Mom would laugh. She never scolded me or forbade me from doing it. At night, I would find her scrubbing my shoes and dabbing them dry—all done with a smile. She endured so much extra work as the price of my enjoyment, but she never resented it. Viviana Mosley was about experiencing life, living a small moment and making it a grand memory that remained long after the moment had passed.

Steven follows my lead and jumps in the puddle, wetting his shoes and pant legs up to his knees. He laughs and jumps again harder, grabbing my hand. We jump together a few times and eventually fall to the ground laughing. I can't remember the last time I've seen him laughing like this, enjoying the moment. We lie on Ms. Maldonado's front lawn until the rain shower has passed. When it has quieted down and all we can hear is a pair of grackles circling the nearby puddle, I turn to look at Steven. His eyes are closed and he's smiling.

"Was that fun?" I ask him.

"Very fun. Can we do it again one day?"

"Sure," I say, not thinking of the baths we both need and the extra load of laundry I'll have to do later. It's something

Mom would've done without regret or second thoughts. I can almost feel her laughter in the gentle breeze that shakes the tree above us, sending more raindrops onto our faces.

"Can we go inside now?" Steven asks.

"Okay." I pull myself up and follow Steven into the house. We leave our shoes by the front entrance, and I tell Steven to leave his clothes in the bathtub when he changes. I could've stayed out there, lying on the wet ground, for the rest of the day. Coming inside and drying off will only lead me directly to so many things that are waiting to get done—chores, home-work, the Etsy shop.

After we eat dinner, I venture into Mom's office. I need to start thinking about my project for the art showcase, and I hope to get inspiration here. I want to do some type of impressionist drawings—something like Degas with the ballerinas. Maybe I could go to Austin to see one of Alexa's dance rehearsals and draw her and the other dancers. The idea floats around in my head but doesn't take root. For one thing, a trip to Austin right now doesn't seem practical. I should probably choose a subject closer to home.

I sit in Mom's desk chair and swivel back and forth, star-ing at her huge twenty-four-by-thirty-six-inch Diego Rivera print. I never understood the appeal of this painting. It's called *Gloriosa Victoria*, and it's horrific. The entire bottom of the painting shows dead children and adults, bathed in blood. There are at least ten dead people—it's like from a war scene or something. Why would she want to put up a painting of dead children?

Mom and I always disagreed about art. To me, this is not beautiful at all. I would send her links to prints I thought she should buy—a lovely Mary Cassatt image of a woman boating, holding a very-much-alive baby, or Claude Monet's two boys in his garden. I lobbied heavily for her to buy one of those to replace the morbid Diego Rivera, but she refused.

I scan the print. There are a bunch of military guys in the center, shaking hands and telling secrets. Bananas are featured prominently in the foreground for some reason, and in the upper right corner are a dozen imprisoned people holding up a flag. Nothing appealing about it.

"Sarah," my dad says from behind me. "I didn't know you were in here."

I swivel around to face him. "Yeah—just thinking." I've tried to focus on anything but what happened last night, yet here he is reminding me of it by just being in the room. I do my best to push past those feelings and think about why I'm in this chair right now. I'm here to be inspired. "I have to pick a theme for an art show I have coming up in December. I've been looking at this picture, trying to figure out why Mom loved it so much."

Dad crosses the room and sits on the small love seat that's positioned between his desk and Mom's. He lets out a long sigh. "It tells an important story. Did she ever explain to you who each of those people represent?"

"I mean, she told me about it, but I don't know if I ever really listened." Admitting this—that I wasn't paying attention when she talked to me about something that mattered to her— is painful. "I know it's about Guatemala."

Dad looks away from me and down at his clasped hands. Everything is quiet for a minute. Eventually he points to the center of the painting, where a man holds a slick silver bomb that has another's man's face on it. "Do you recognize that man's face on the bomb?"

I stand up and lean across the desk to look closely. "He looks familiar, but I don't know any of the Guatemalan guys."

"Well, he's not Guatemalan. That's President Eisenhower."

I look at my dad. "The 'I like Ike' guy?" I can picture his campaign buttons from my history textbooks.

"Yeah, and the man holding the bomb was the secretary of state at the time, John Foster Dulles."

I look closely at the guy with the bomb. He wears glasses and a camo-type outfit. One hand rests on the bomb while the other shakes the hand of a rat-faced man with a moustache. "Like Dulles Airport in DC?"

"Yes, the airport was named after him."

"Why are these American men in a picture about Guatemala?"

"Well, in 1954, Dulles's brother—who's whispering in his ear there—was head of the CIA, and they led a coup to overthrow the president of Guatemala."

"Whoa." I don't remember hearing about this before. "So who's the rat-faced guy?"

Dad's eyes dart back to the picture. "Rat-faced guy?"

I point at the man in the very center. "The one with the gun in his pants and wads of cash in his pocket?"

Dad laughs as he gets another look and sees what I'm talking about. "That's Carlos Castillo Armas. He's the dictator the US helped put in power, in place of the ousted president."

I can barely believe we're having an actual conversation. He's always loved talking about history, but this is the first time he's brought it up with me in six months. "I still don't understand why Mom liked this piece," I say. "I mean, look at those children at their feet. Dead, bloody, dismembered. Art is supposed to be beautiful. This isn't beautiful."

"It's the reality of what happened. Thousands of people were executed when Castillo Armas came into power. Art can be beautiful, but your mom always said that to her, art was about having a voice. A voice to tell important stories." He glances toward his desk and folds his arms across his chest. I wonder how hard it is for him to talk about her right now. I think this is the most we've talked about her since she died.

I sink back into the swivel chair. "She always wanted me to pay attention to stuff like this." I should've taken more time to look at what she wanted to show me, but I don't say that.

"She wanted you to understand that this is part of your history. Your great-grandpa Eugenio left Guatemala not long after this happened. The new government was executing dissidents and intellectuals. He went to Mexico and started a life there, met your great-grandma Maria."

I swivel around to face my dad. "But if this new government was so bad, why did the US support it?" I remember learning that before Eisenhower became president, he was a general who helped the Allies win World War II. I can't wrap my head around why someone who fought the Nazis—and this Dulles guy who had a whole airport named after him—would be involved with these terrible things in Guatemala.

"It was the Cold War," he says like that explains anything. He's forgetting I'm not one of his college students.

"What does that mean?" I press.

He shrugs. "Americans were terrified of communism. They were suspicious of any leader who embraced what they considered to be communist ideas—like redistributing wealth or making it harder for private companies to do whatever they wanted."

"This is wild. We've learned a little about the Cold War in history but there was never any mention of Guatemala."

"For a long time, this stuff was a state secret. It wasn't until certain CIA documents were declassified in the nineties that it became public knowledge."

"Okay, but that's still way before I was born."

Dad nods. "It's not the kind of history a lot of Americans feel comfortable confronting. I'm glad you're asking about this, though. Your mom really wanted you to have a good understanding of it, of why art like this was so important to her." He's now scanning the room, looking for something, probably wondering if he brought a bottle in here.

"This is the kind of stuff she taught in her classes?"

He nods, gets up, and walks over to his desk, still searching. "Yeah, one of the classes she taught was on US relations with Latin America. There are a lot of other examples besides Guatemala." Not finding what he's looking for, he gives up and walks over to her bookcase. "This is her notebook." He plucks a thick spiral-bound volume from the top shelf. "She wrote a lot in here about her classes, her thoughts, art. She said it was easier to organize her thoughts on paper than on a computer. Maybe you could read through it. Get some ideas."

I take the notebook from him. "I think I will. Thanks, Dad."

"She has a couple of other books in here. Rina Lazo. Frida Kahlo." He points in the general direction of Mom's bookshelf. Before I can respond, he leaves the room.

A short conversation with me was too much for him. It brought back too many memories of her, of what was important to her, of what he loved and will always love about her. I wonder if we'll ever be able to talk about her without him finding it unbearable.

CHAPTER FIFTEEN

I don't open Mom's notebook over the weekend. The conversation with Dad, the memories of my indifference to her perspective, have filled me with guilt. I think about the missed opportunities to have conversations that were important to her. I have her notebook, but I could've let her share those thoughts with me with her voice if I had just taken the time to listen, instead of always thinking that I knew best, that I knew more, that she was just being a mom. I leave the notebook on my desk, promising myself I'll make time to look at it this week.

On Monday we have our first field trip to Las Positas Elementary for COOP. We're going to observe a fifth-grade science lab and a PE class. We'll come back another day for math, art, and music classes. Makaila and I share a seat near the front of the bus. She's wearing a *Black Girls in STEM* T-shirt.

David pulls Carlos into the seat across from us. "Hi, Sarah," David says, pulling a hoodie over his head.

"Hi. You excited to see what the PE class will be like?" I ask him.

He pats down the back of his head, settling down a few tufts of hair that came up when he pulled the hoodie over it. "Yeah! Since I'm going to be the first one from COOP to lead a class, I need to get ideas. I'm curious to know what kind of music they use for the warm-ups. Like, it has to be songs the kids know and like, but you have to be careful with lyrics. And sometimes kids get tired of the same old songs over and over."

"So, you're making plans for your presentation already?"

"Yeah, I got a little playlist going." David hands me his phone across the aisle, and I scroll through about ten songs.

"Are you nervous about teaching?"

"Nah. PE is so much fun. You just have to let kids get out there and enjoy themselves. Make it a bullying-free space where everyone can feel like a winner. That's the key."

"You'll do great," I say, handing back his phone. He flashes a smile that I wish I could capture to look at whenever I feel sad or lonely.

Carlos takes away David's attention, and I turn to Makaila, who's scrolling through her own phone. "What do you think, Sarah? Can third graders get into a sink-or-float science project or is that more for lower grades?"

"I don't know . . . maybe lower grades."

"How about magnets or taking the temperature of different substances?"

"My brother is in third grade. I can ask him what he thinks might be more interesting."

Makaila brightens and looks up. "Oh, that's great. Do you think I could come over to your place and practice my class with him?"

"Sure," I tell her. "Just let me know when."

When we get to the first class, which is in the science lab of Las Positas, Makaila goes right to the front to take notes on how the teacher handles everything. I stay toward the back, out of the way, and David comes to stand right next to me.

He signals behind us. "I have to stay near the eyewash station in case of emergencies."

I look over my shoulder at an emergency station that has probably never been used. "Funny, but I think you will be okay." I look up at his eyes and hope nothing in the world ever happens to them.

The teacher is in his twenties, and he has all of his students' attention. I'm in awe of how every butt in this class is firmly planted on a lab stool. These tall metal stools are ripe for misbehavior, but the kids have clearly been trained on how to behave in a lab.

I watch the teacher, thinking about how I might manage a class one day. Art class seems full of opportunities for kids to act out or get distracted. But that's kind of a hypocritical thought, since I'm having a hard time listening to this teacher when David is right next to me.

I like him, and he likes me. I can tell from the way his dancing eyes intermittently go from the teacher to me, and from the curve of his lip when he catches me looking back at him.

But as soon as I start to imagine reaching out to graze his fingers in this moment, maybe kissing him one day, I remember how our first date ended.

I shift my weight to my right foot, increasing the space between David and me. I refocus my attention on the teacher and suddenly wish I had followed Makaila to the front of the room.

On the way back to Richards, Makaila and I end up at the back of the bus while David and Carlos keep their seats up front.

At home, I try to put away all thoughts of David as I scramble to throw dinner together. A very hungry Steven stands beside me near the stove, tapping his foot and glancing repeatedly at the clock on the microwave, as if that will magically make the macaroni and cheese cook faster. I finish stirring the powdered cheese and milk in the pan and scoop it into the two bowls that Steven impatiently holds in front of me.

"Why are you getting two bowls?" I ask him.

"One's for Dad," he says, turning to leave. "We're eating up in his room. The game's about to start."

I think about following Steven upstairs to see if Dad is even awake and actually going to watch whatever game this is. What if he's just passed out on his bed or in the recliner?

Setting aside that worry, I take the pan to the table and grab a spoon to eat the rest of the macaroni and cheese. No point of dishing it out into a bowl—that would just be another dish to wash.

With Steven and Dad presumably occupied, I can properly fixate on something besides the two of them. My mind automatically and happily jumps to David.

Friends. We're friends. Friends can text each other. I could very well text David right now if I wanted to. I unlock my phone as I take another bite of the macaroni and cheese. I hover over our last text conversation, the one about the Astros game.

SARAH: Hey, Steven was asking about seeing your baseball card albums.

A lie, but a believable one. I don't have to wait long for a response.

DAVID: I could bring them by tomorrow. I'm sure he's busy watching the World Series right now.

Yes, the World Series. Tonight must be Game One. I hope David doesn't see through my lie, wondering why Steven would be asking about the baseball cards when his attention is elsewhere at the moment.

SARAH: Yes, he's watching it right now, so tomorrow would be good.

DAVID: I can come by after basketball practice?

SARAH: Sounds good

He responds with a smiling emoji, and I'm thankful for baseball for the first time ever.

CHAPTER SIXTEEN

Against all my best judgment and soundest discipline, I've invited David over to show Steven his baseball cards. David has become a good friend to Steven, so this isn't entirely selfish on my part. As long as I don't think of David as anything more than a friend. Or at least, even if I do think of him as something more, I can't allow my feelings to permeate the world outside my mind. Now is not the time for me; it is time for my family. That's what I keep telling myself right up until I hear the knock on the door.

I hop up. Steven is ahead of me and lets David in. David's eyes leap to me; I smile and remind myself why he has to remain a good friend.

Steven grabs for the albums David holds in his hands. "Can I see?"

David follows Steven over to the couch and places the albums on the floor by his feet. I sit on the other side of Steven.

"You have Barry Bonds?" Steven says as he flips the page to read the info on the back of the card. "And Bagwell. Alex Rodriguez. Roger Clemens. Wait! When did you get this old Nolan Ryan one?"

Steven continues calling out names and turning pages. David just sits there patiently, responding to Steven's questions on the rare occasions when Steven pauses long enough to hear an answer. I sit back to take it all in.

When we finish the second album, Steven reaches for the third one, but it's empty. "This one doesn't have any cards," Steven says.

"It's for you. You can put some of your cards in there if you want," David says.

"Really?" Steven flips the empty pocketed pages. "I can have it?"

"Yep. Now, I know you like to keep some of yours in stacks, so don't feel like you have to put them in here if you don't want. I just thought that maybe you'd like to put some of your favorites in here."

"Yeah!" Steven stands up and takes the album with him.

"Steven," I say before he leaves the room. "What do you say?"

"Thank you, David," he says, turning around.

"You're welcome."

Steven scrambles up the stairs and slams his door shut. There is a space on the couch now between David and me.

I hop up from the couch. "You want a snack?"

"Sure." He follows me into the kitchen.

I hand him a water bottle and a bag of Doritos. He leans against the counter as he opens the bag. "I'm really glad you texted last night. I figured I could count on Steven to keep pestering you until you invited me."

I hold my own Doritos bag at eye level, pretending to read the ingredients. But when I look up, every doubt I've had about taking that next step with David disappears. There is no one in the kitchen; there are no distractions. Just him. Just me. "Actually, I lied. He didn't ask about you or the albums."

He puts his Doritos bag on the counter, the interest in his eyes sharpening as he looks at me. "Oh. Why did you lie?"

I open my bag and take out a triangle. I shrug, pretending I'm not completely filled with anxiety. "I just really wanted you to come over."

The slow spread of his smile mirrors the stretching of all the nerves in my stomach. He inches closer. I drop my Doritos bag on the counter, wishing I could wipe the orange powder off my fingers before I slide them toward him, centimeters away from his waist.

His movements are slow, deliberate, as if he wants to ensure he does everything correctly. He puts his right hand on my cheek, tentatively, and I lean in to it. His other hand comes around my shoulder and stops at the base of my neck. He bends his head toward me, and I can feel his warm breath on my cheek. His lips press against my cheek. The pressure is so soft and so faint, yet I feel the effects tingle all the way down my spine to my legs. He kisses my cheek again with more pressure and turns my face gently to find my lips. My arm goes around his shoulder, and I pull him in tighter.

It's exactly the kiss I expected from him—gentle, soft, slow. It is not demanding, overbearing, or greedy. He doesn't take more than I'm willing to give. When I open my eyes, his forehead is pressed against mine, his eyes closed.

He exhales slowly. "How'd I do?"

"What do you mean?"

"The painting on your phone case—the way the man kisses the woman . . . I was aiming for that."

"It was perfect," I say. "You're a great kisser. Someone should paint a portrait of you kissing."

He leans in again. This time, his hands don't frame my

face. They drop down to my waist, and I wrap my arms around his neck. He pulls me in so close that I can feel his ribs, his heart racing against mine. For the first time, I am glad that Dad is probably passed out in bed and won't be walking in on us.

CHAPTER SEVENTEEN

As we board the school bus taking us to Las Positas Elementary School, Makaila raises her eyebrows in David's direction. He's right behind me. I told her at lunch that David kissed me. After I claim a seat, she waits in the aisle to see what he'll do. David pauses, looks at Makaila with a question in his eyes. She shrugs and points to the spot next to me, which he quickly slides into after smiling at her. Makaila sits behind me, and Carlos sits next to her, since he's also been left without a seatmate.

David leaves a slim space between us. There's definitely plenty of room on his other side. I vow to close the remaining distance between us before we reach the school. I adjust my shoulder slightly so it touches his and put my hand in a spot so close to his that I can almost feel the dark hairs on the back of his hand. He recognizes my cue and takes my hand, interlacing his fingers with mine. I smile up at him, and he leans in to rest his forehead on my temple. I breathe him in, the simple smell of a boy, the gentle air coming from his mouth, the possibility of later, of his lips against mine.

I want more of this. A lot more of this. "Want to come over to study for the physics test after school?"

"Yeah. Right after school?"

"If you're not busy."

"We don't have practice today, so yeah, after school is perfect."

David parks his Jeep in front of my house as I park my car in the driveway. The faint sound of Robert's trimmer buzzes down the street, but I don't look for him. I focus on the door, hoping Dad is upstairs and unaware that I'm bringing a boy home.

Most of my dating was done at PFA, without my parents looking over my shoulder. I dated a few boys here when I was home for the summer, mostly double dates that Alexa set up, but nothing that serious. Dad's been nice to David, and I'm sure he would be okay with me bringing him home, but I don't really want to deal with anything Dad has to say about it right now.

As I open the door, Steven's and Dad's voices drift from the kitchen. They're talking about the World Series, and it suddenly occurs to me that Steven hasn't been rehashing its details ad nauseam to me. I'm grateful he's able to talk to Dad about it.

I grab David's hand and hurry us up the stairs. I close my bedroom door behind us and listen to see if either Steven or Dad call for me.

"Is your Dad okay that I'm in your room with the door closed?" David clutches his backpack, ready to retreat.

"He doesn't care."

"Are you sure?" he doesn't move. Not an inch.

"I'm sure. I promise." I lead him to my bed. We sit down with our backs to the wall and both dig into our backpacks, pulling out our copies of the review packet that Lemmon gave us. "Lemmon is very thorough, I see."

David leafs through the packet and whistles. "So, you want to read over it and then we can quiz each other?"

"Sure, or we can make flash cards." I get up and open the top drawer of my desk to grab a plastic-wrapped package of index cards.

David grins. "Flash cards?"

"It was just a suggestion." I leave the cards on the desk and sit back down next to him, this time so close that I can feel the seam of his jeans against my leggings.

He sets down the review packet and slides his hand up to my jaw, pushing back my hair. He leans in to kiss me, his soft lips pressing against mine. I curve my arm around his back to feel the muscles across the broad expanse of his shoulders. Gently, I push against him until he lies back on my bed. His arm goes fully around me while his other hand finds my hip and gives it a soft squeeze. His thumb rubs across the waistband of my leggings, and the slight touch reverberates from my toes all the way up to my neck.

We turn to our sides, pressing ourselves against each other. My arms wrap around his neck, and I reach my hand into his hair, running my fingers through the soft waves. His kisses move from my lips to my neck, and he shifts my hair aside to find space for his mouth.

My phone dings with an incoming text. I pull away from David, grab my phone off the desk, and lie back down. My head rests right in the crook of David's shoulder and neck. He kisses my forehead and runs his fingers up and down my arm while I check my messages.

"My dad just sent me a text." When was the last time he did that? Is it possible that he did see us walk in, knows we're up here making out, and actually has a problem with it?

DAD: Just remembered. Your mom has a photo album in the office. It has a lot of old photos of Guatemala taken by your great-grandfather. You can get some ideas for your project.

"Oh." Relieved that this isn't a scolding, I turn to David. "I mentioned my art show to him, and he says there's a photo album that might give me some ideas. Want to check it out with me?"

"Sure." We head downstairs to the office. I can hear Dad's TV droning, so I know he's in his room now.

"It's probably on her shelves." I scan all three rows of Mom's bookcase, but I don't find a photo album. "Will you look in that file cabinet?" I tell David.

He opens the top drawer while I scan the two drawers of her desk. Nothing. I look around the room.

On top of her bookcase there's a clay pot, and next to that is a light wooden box. I bring the wooden box down. It has decorative carvings on the outside, and when I open the thick hinged lid, I discover a small album. It has space for only a single photograph on each page. I bring the album over to the love seat and open it. David sits next to me and puts his arm around me, and I lean into him so we can both see the black-and-white photographs.

The first photograph shows a city square with a large volcano looming in the background. I slip it out of its plastic sleeve. The writing on the back says *Antigua*. I turn the page to a photograph of a large, ornate white building. This one's labeled *Palacio Nacional*. The third photo is of a group of people holding up a large sign that reads "Viva Árbenz." Next is an image of men in button-down shirts and linen pants, wearing hats and holding rifles. The back of the photo says *tropas en un camion*.

David pulls out his phone and does a quick search. "It means *troops in a truck*."

"Ah, thanks. My couple months of Spanish class did not help me translate that."

There are other photographs of workers loading bananas onto train cars, bananas stacked on the ground with workers gathered around them, an airplane flying over a plaza.

I don't know what's up with all these bananas, but I tell David everything my dad told me about the CIA's coup in Guatemala.

"That's intense. And the DC airport is really named after those Dulles guys?" he asks.

"Well, one of them. I forget which one."

The last photo is a headshot of a man with a neatly trimmed moustache and dark black hair. On the back of his picture is the name *Eugenio Alvarado*.

"My great-grandfather," I tell David. "My dad said he left Guatemala after the coup because his life was in danger. He went to Mexico, married my great-grandmother, and never went back to Guatemala."

"Why was he in danger?" David asks.

"My dad said that the dictator who took over the country killed a bunch of people who didn't agree with the new government. I want to research it more." I look again at the photograph of my great-grandfather. "I think this is what I want to do for my art project—draw him and the things he witnessed. I think I need to tell his story."

He leans in closer to look at Eugenio's picture. "I think that would be really cool."

Tucked into the same sleeve that held this photo is a lined piece of paper with writing on both sides. It's written in impossible-to-read Spanish cursive. "Maybe Señora Dominguez can help me with this." I put the album and the letter back in the decorative box and we take it to my room.

David grabs the package of index cards off my desk and sits down on my bed, leaning against the headboard. "I can make us some flash cards to study for the test, if you want to start drawing right now." He tears off the plastic wrapping, takes out a pen, and writes a label on the first card. I look forward to studying the cards later, examining his handwriting, and wondering why he doesn't cross his *t*'s. I watch him for a minute more, and he looks at me and winks.

I sit at my desk and turn to a new page on my sketch pad. I study the photograph of Eugenio Alvarado, my great-grandfather. I begin sketching his face, trying to capture his look of stern concentration. I wonder what he was thinking at the precise moment this photograph was taken. Was this right after he left Guatemala? I stare at his eyes, searching for any familiarity. He is, after all, my relative. But nothing in his face feels familiar to me. He seems so far away right now. I want to understand him—what he's missing, what he's hoping for—so that I can get the look on his face just right.

"How are the flash cards coming along?" I ask David after a while.

"Good. We're going to ace this test." He turns to me, head on my pillow. "How's the drawing?"

"It's okay." I look down at my work so far and don't feel ready to share it. "I'll show you when I'm done." I'll finish it later, when I'm alone and ready to contemplate the emotions on Eugenio's face that I can't quite understand. Right now, I'm not able to give him and the drawing my full attention. I get up and move toward my bed as David makes room for me. I climb in next to him and he pulls me in for more kissing.

CHAPTER EIGHTEEN

My ten-minute conference with Ms. Escamilla starts at 4:15, so I rush out of eighth period and walk the entire length of the school to the art room.

"Hi, Sarah." Ms. Escamilla gestures to one of the large black tables. "Sit down. Talk to me about your theme."

"I want to draw some of the images in these pictures." I show her the album and my half-completed drawing of Eugenio Alvarado, hastily explaining some of the context. "I want to tell the story of the Guatemala coup from my great-grandfather's point of view."

Mrs. Escamilla takes off her glasses to examine the photographs and my work-in-progress. "Okay, well, this is a wonderful start, Sarah. How many pieces do you plan on presenting?"

"Maybe ten or twelve; I don't know yet."

"Part of the showcase will be explaining how you are personally connected to your work."

"Well, my great-grandfather left Guatemala right before its civil war. He was outspoken against the new government, and was afraid he would be killed, so he moved to Mexico and never went back."

"That's certainly good information to present. Still, you need to make sure to touch on how this all impacts you directly as an artist. So, just keep that in mind as you're working. We'll meet again in a week or two to check on your progress."

"Okay, thank you."

"Thank *you*, Sarah. This is really great work. I'm looking forward to seeing how it all comes together."

I think about Ms. Escamilla's words as I drive home. How has any of this impacted me personally? It hasn't, I don't think.

Steven is up in Dad's room reading him the sports page. I go into my room, grab my mom's notebook, and settle onto my bed. I'm ready now. I need to know everything she thought and believed about this issue in particular. It is now *my* issue, my theme for my first art show.

On the first page, she's taped a postcard-sized copy of the same Diego Rivera print she has in her office, *Gloriosa Victoria*. Glorious Victory. I guess the coup was considered glorious by those who overthrew the president. What was his name again? I scan her notes. Jacobo Árbenz. Why did President Eisenhower want to overthrow him? The Cold War, Dad said. I thought the Cold War was against the Soviet Union; what does that have to do with Guatemala?

In her journal, Mom has handwritten notes, plus photocopied quotes from books with their citations.

After half an hour of reading, I basically understand that the US was fighting communism, and they thought President Árbenz was a communist. He supported labor unions and wanted to redistribute land to Guatemala's Indigenous people. I guess this, in the eyes of the US government, made him a problem.

Mom has three pages full of notes about a US company called the United Fruit Company that was operating in Guatemala. As I start to skim through this section I notice that there's a paperclip hooked over the edge of a later page. I flip to that spot and find a flyer clipped into place. A flyer with Mom's photo.

It advertises a lecture at UTSA, featuring my mom. She's pictured in a dark maroon turtleneck sweater, her curls framing her face. Her lecture is called "Rotten Fruit." I do a search on YouTube for *Viviana Mosley* and *rotten fruit*. There's a four-minute clip from her lecture, and I click on it.

The video starts part of the way through her talk. She's standing at a podium in a large lecture hall that's almost full. She's wearing her favorite black suit—pencil skirt and fitted jacket. She slips her dark-rimmed reading glasses off her face and holds them in her hand as she speaks.

"They owned much of the land and employed many people. They were opposed to most of the reforms that Árbenz proposed. So they lobbied the US to overthrow him. Both the Dulles brothers had done legal work for the United Fruit Company, and Allen Dulles was on the company's board of directors. The husband of Eisenhower's secretary was a lobbyist for the company. A lot of people in Eisenhower's administration had links to the company, and they stood to lose a lot of money if Árbenz followed through with these policies."

I turn back to look at the Rivera print. I see the US dollars in Rat Face's jacket again. One of the Dulles brothers has a bag full of money hanging from his shoulder.

In the video, my mom talks about the thirty-six-year civil war and genocide that followed the coup, the hundreds of thousands of people who were killed or "disappeared." How the US trained and equipped security forces in Guatemala that led to the mass killings of Mayans. How dictator after dictator seized power over the decades, and the US supported each one. Mom's words are matter-of-fact, but emotion bleeds into her voice as she speaks.

I find it hard to imagine a civil war lasting thirty-six years. And it all seems to have started with the coup in 1954.

Once the video clip ends, I go back to reading Mom's notes. After the CIA put Rat Face into power, he had a bunch of opposition leaders arrested and more than a thousand farmers killed. One of the Dulles brothers—I honestly can't tell them apart—told Rat Face to detain people trying to leave the country. This is when the forced disappearances in Guatemala started. I wonder how my great-grandfather managed to escape. He must've gotten very lucky. Staying in Guatemala probably would've meant imprisonment or death. I think about how he could have been one of the "disappeared," how his "disappearance" would have meant I wouldn't be here right now.

I think about our American ideals, our First Amendment right to speak freely. How hypocritical for the Dulles brothers to support the incarceration of people with opposing views while they enjoyed those freedoms here in the US. Their backing of a murderous dictator tore up a little country in ways it's never recovered from. It seems so un-American to name a huge airport in Washington, DC, after a guy who was basically a war criminal—but on the other hand it actually seems like a very American thing to do.

As I read my mom's notes, I sense her anger at what history has left us with. I look at Diego Rivera's painting again. It is still not pleasing, not what I've always considered to be pretty art, but he was probably not in a mood to make something pretty. He was angry, and he wanted to show this to the world. The bound bodies. The mutilated bodies. The bullet-riddled bodies. The bloodied bodies of children. The dismembered child right next to Eisenhower's face.

The indignation of this artist I've never cared for—the

indignation my mother shared—slowly seeps into me, but I don't know where to direct my feelings. I set aside the journal. I close my eyes and picture my favorite paintings: Monet's garden with its colorful irises. The soft pastels of Mary Cassatt's lilacs in the window. The gold shades in *The Kiss*. I focus on those images, trying to cleanse my mind of all the devastation.

A notification for a text comes in, and I'm grateful for the distraction. It's David. A wonderful distraction.

DAVID: Hey, I'm kinda nervous about my presentation.

SARAH: Really? I've never seen you nervous. You always seem so cool.

DAVID: You've seen me nervous. I just hide it well.

SARAH: When have you been nervous?

DAVID: When I kissed you. Super nervous.

SARAH: Ha! I couldn't tell.

DAVID: You busy? Can I come over and show you and Steven my playlist for tomorrow? I'm scared the kids won't be into it and won't want to do the workout.

SARAH: Yeah, come over.

DAVID: Can I bring a pizza?

SARAH: Steven would love you!

DAVID: How about you?

SARAH: I love pizza too. :P

DAVID: Okay, see you in a few.

About an hour later, David is setting a pizza box on our kitchen table. Steven has two plates in his hands before David can even lift the lid off the pizza.

"Thanks, David. Sarah, can I eat upstairs with Dad? We're supposed to go over tomorrow's lineup."

"Sure, but David wanted us to listen to the music he's going to use tomorrow in his PE class."

Steven balances the pizza slices on the two plates in his hands. "Okay, I'll come down in half an hour." He rushes out of the room and stomps up the stairs.

David says, "So, your dad is doing okay?"

I grab a slice of pizza and nod. "Yeah, I think so. We haven't had any . . . episodes lately. Steven's been spending a lot of time with him, watching the World Series, so I think that helps."

"Yeah, tomorrow is a big game."

"Then they'll be watching."

After we finish our pizza, David and I go out to the living room to wait for Steven. I fold my legs under me and scoot closer to him on the couch. "Are you nervous now?" I ask.

He covers his eyes with his hand and looks at me between his fingers. "Maybe."

I lean in, and he closes the gap between us. His hands go to my face, and I wrap my arms around his neck, pulling him to me. His kiss is still gentle but eager. He kisses my neck, and I let my body relax at his touch.

Steven's feet plod down the stairs, and we pull away from each other. He is prompt as always: thirty minutes exactly.

David shows us his playlist for the PE class's workout tomorrow. He also explains a game he'll play with the students called "Frogs Across the Pond." Steven declares the game to be very fun while labeling the playlist okay, nothing to write home about. David laughs at that verdict.

"Good luck tomorrow. I have to go." Steven flies out of the room, his duty completed.

I feel immense gratitude for baseball—the reason my father and brother are occupied this evening, the reason I now get to sit next to this good-looking boy who's leaning in to kiss me.

CHAPTER NINETEEN

David is as cool as a cucumber when we walk into the elementary school's gym. He says he gets nervous, but I don't see it at all. Nothing but relaxed vibes bounce off of him. I wish him good luck, and he gives me a smile and a hand squeeze before he heads to the front of the room, carrying himself like he's already in charge of this expansive area and its sixty-five tiny occupants.

Makaila and I sit in the rear of the gym, our backs against the wall. I compliment her shirt, which says *STEM is the New Black*, before I pull my sketch pad out of my backpack. I want to record David's mastery of this moment. He introduces himself and gives the fourth graders a few instructions. After he starts his playlist, the students stand up and mimic his movements.

Makaila looks down at my sketchbook and rolls her eyes playfully. "You are smitten."

I smile and shrug because maybe I am. I give myself permission to stare at David's legs beneath his black athletic shorts as he moves from side to side with the music. I am, after all, drawing him, so I have to stare. He does double jumping jacks, and the fourth graders follow suit. He does a little clapping thing with his hands above his head, one foot tapping with the rhythm. He launches into a series of moves that are fairly simple for the fourth graders to copy, but they're so hypnotic that I can't look away. I'm having an inner struggle between wanting to watch every single one of his muscles move with the music and feeling the need to capture him on paper.

After about ten minutes of music-accompanied exercises, David explains the rules of the game the kids will play and breaks them into small groups.

"So, is this thing with you and David serious?" Makaila asks me.

"I don't know. I mean, I really like him and we've been hanging out a lot. But things have been complicated at home since my mom died. I have to help take care of my brother and that doesn't leave a lot of time for a relationship."

"That sounds really hard. I'm sorry."

"David is understanding, though. So we'll see."

"Is it still okay for me to come over tonight to see which experiment your brother likes for my class presentation?"

"Yeah, for sure. I already told him about it. Just be prepared—he's kind of an opinionated kid."

She laughs. "That's okay. I need opinions. I want to rock my class, like David is doing. Look at your man. He's got those kids so excited to play this game."

I watch as groups of students take turns tossing plastic rings in front of teammates, who jump from ring to ring across the room. David circulates among the groups, encouraging kids and helping them along as they play. He's in his element. He catches me watching and gives me a quick wink as he continues to move around this space that he now owns.

Dad is upstairs rewatching the same baseball documentary he's seen a thousand times. I guess there's comfort in the familiar. I've lured Steven away from Dad's room with a promise of dinner in front of *SportsCenter* in the living room instead of at the table.

Makaila shows up carrying a huge tub, with her heavy backpack strapped to her shoulders. "Girl, I came prepared. Your brother better like one of these."

I laugh, but I sure hope he does. She brings all her stuff to the kitchen, and I call Steven in. I introduce Makaila to him, and he sits across from her at the table. She lays out some materials in front of him: a rubber duck, a marble, a cork, a Popsicle stick, a rock, a dime, and a ping-pong ball.

"So, Steven. This experiment is about density. The density of an object will determine whether it will sink or float. So—"

Steven eyes the neat row of items before him. He points to each one as he says, "Float, sink, float, float, sink, sink, float."

"Steven, let her finish."

Makaila scrunches her lips.

He shrugs. "Sarah, you said she was going to do an experiment. This isn't an experiment when you already know the results."

Makaila crosses her arms. "Actually, it is still an experiment. What you just said was your hypothesis. Scientists make educated guesses, which you just did, but then they have to test their hypotheses to see if they're correct."

"Okay, but this is for little kids, like first or second grade."

"Well, I have a backup activity. Maybe you'll like this one better." Makaila puts her sink-or-float items back in the tub. "What do you know about mixtures and solutions?"

"I know what a mixture is," Steven says. "It's different

things put together." He gives Makaila a pensive look. "A solution is like the contact lens solution my mom would use to wash her contact lenses, right?"

"Yeah, something like that. A solution is a type of mixture that can't be easily separated. Let's look at a few." Makaila pulls out four plastic containers. She lifts the lid off the first one and pushes it toward Steven.

Steven's eyes widen as he sees M&Ms and peanuts.

"Yes, you can have them," Makaila says, laughing at his unasked question. "But first you have to separate this mixture."

Steven uses his fingers to separate the M&Ms from the peanuts. Next Makaila shows him a container full of paper clips and rocks, which Steven separates with a magnet she gives him. He separates sand from water with a coffee filter.

"This last mixture is also a solution," Makaila explains to him. She has Steven stir salt into water until it dissolves. "Let's see if you can separate it."

He makes a few attempts with a strainer and a coffee filter but is unable to separate the salt from the water.

"Let's try one last thing." Makaila takes a hot plate out of her tub and plugs it in. "Let's see if boiling the solution will separate it."

She has Steven pour the salt water into a little pan and then she turns the heat on. We wait a few minutes and watch as the water boils. The water evaporates, leaving behind clumps of salt.

"Wow!" Steven says. "Is that salt?"

"Yeah, that's the only way to separate the salt from the water. So solutions *can* be separated; it's just harder than separating a simple mixture."

"Can I taste it to see if it's actually the salt?"

Makaila uses tongs to pick up a clump of salt, which she places in Steven's outstretched hand.

He licks it. "Yeah, this is a winner, Makaila. Your class will like this one. It's cool."

"Thanks, Steven. I'm glad you liked it."

"Can I go show Dad this salt, Sarah?"

"Do you still need him?" I ask Makaila.

"No, I think I'm good."

Steven scampers off with the salt, plus the plastic container of M&Ms and peanuts.

"Thanks for lending me your brother. He's very picky about his experiments, so I'm flattered that he liked the second one."

"He's very picky about a lot of things."

"Well, I feel a lot better about tomorrow. I'm still really nervous, though."

"You'll do great. That was a very cool experiment. The kids will love it."

"I hope so. You know, elementary is not my preference. I want to teach a high school chemistry class. AP Chemistry. Students who really care, you know? This little-kid stuff is hard. How's your lesson coming?"

"I haven't even thought about it. I've been spending a lot of time on my art show project. I don't even know what I'm going to do when I have to take my turn teaching."

"Well, at least you have your brother to try some things with."

"Yeah, he'll be free with his opinions, that's for sure."

Makaila puts lids on her containers. "So, what is your art show about?"

I tell her the basic premise about using my voice to tell the story of what happened to Guatemala.

"That's really messed up. But honestly, if you think about how the US has historically benefitted from oppressing other groups, it's not that surprising."

"I know. It makes me so mad, though. Like, how can they name a huge airport after a guy who helped to overthrow a democratically elected president and put such a terrible person in power?"

"Girl, they've been doing that type of stuff as a habit. Like, you know there's a high school not too far from here named after Robert E. Lee."

"Yeah, that's a fair point. I think what gets me about the Guatemala stuff is that I'm just now learning about it. We don't cover any of this in school. We're never taught about how the US has intervened in these other countries, even paid for and supported genocide."

"They've been getting away with genocide in *this* country since day one. Why wouldn't they try it in other countries too?" She lets her lips form a tiny smile. "You're right that they don't teach us that in school, though. I think your art show is going to be really cool. This is stuff people need to hear. Have you started the artwork?"

"I have one piece that I'm working on." I retrieve the half-finished sketch of my great-grandfather from my backpack.

She studies my drawing for a minute. "Sarah, this is so good. You really catch his emotions."

"Thanks. That's my goal." I help Makaila finish packing everything she brought and walk her to her car. I think about what she said about Robert E. Lee High School. I remember hearing something a while ago about a petition to rename the school. What happened with that?

After Makaila leaves, I package up Skipper's mom's portraits and stick the prepaid shipping label on the envelope. I'll have to drop it off tomorrow on my way to school. It took so much time and so many angry emails from Skipper's mom for me to finally finish. I have no idea how I'll fill my remaining orders. I know a lot of customers want their portraits before Christmas as gifts, but how will I find time when I need to focus on my art project? On the other hand, if I prioritize the art show over my Etsy sales, how will I have enough grocery and gas money?

Drawing portraits for strangers so I can afford groceries is not the choice I want to make. It would not be the choice I'd have to make if Mom was still here. The thought brings tears to my eyes, but I have no time to cry.

CHAPTER TWENTY

I t's the quintessential high school experience. David is holding my hand, and we're walking down the hall to physics. People who know him but don't really know me stare, and David gives them friendly nods. I guess it's official. We haven't really said the words—boyfriend, girlfriend—but that's essentially what we are now that we're holding hands for all of Richards High School to see.

We slide into desks next to each other.

"My friend Bobby is having a birthday party on Sunday. His parents rented out like half of Top Golf. Will you come with me?" In a rush he adds, "Brad's not going to be there, in case you're wondering about that. He and Bobby don't hang out."

"I'm liking Bobby more and more," I joke. But I'm stalling, weighing whether to accept the invitation.

It would be a real date, not just hanging out at my house. I remember our previous date, with its ruinous ending. David's bright, expectant eyes wait for an answer, and I want to tell him yes. I want to go on a date with this guy who I'm pretty sure is my boyfriend, but memories of my dad drunkenly driving my car lurk in the back of my mind.

"And if you're worried about Steven, we can bring him.

I bet he'll want to see Game Seven. Bobby's going to have them play the game on the big screens there."

"I think Steven and my dad are planning on watching the game at home. Steven made me a long grocery list of all the game snacks they'll need." Dad and Steven will be upstairs in Dad's room for like four hours. I should be okay to leave them. "So they'll be fine. I can go with you."

A smile spreads across David's face. "Okay, good, but are you sure?"

I nod, feeling a matching smile spread on my face. "Yeah, it sounds like fun."

As class starts, I text Alexa.

SARAH: I think I have a boyfriend now.

She texts back a row of emojis with hearts as eyes.

At the end of the day, I go to Señora Dominguez's classroom. I've asked if she'll help me translate the letter I found. She said I could come by after school.

"Hola, Señora Dominguez." I enter her classroom and take the empty chair by her desk. "Thanks for taking the time for this."

"I'm happy to help. Tell me what you have here."

I hand her the letter. "I can't read any of this. I think my great-grandfather may have written it, but I'm not sure. I found it with some old photographs."

She examines the letter. "It's addressed to someone named Viviana . . ."

"That's my mom."

"And it's signed by Eugenio Alvarado."

"Yes, my great-grandfather. He was from Guatemala originally."

"And there's a date." She points to a series of numbers at the top of the letter. "It's written in the Spanish format, with the day first and the month second."

I scan the date and do some mental math. This was probably when my mom was in grad school.

Señora Dominguez reads the letter out loud in Spanish a few sentences at a time and translates as she goes. "He explains that he was a photographer for a small newspaper in the capital. He's probably referring to Guatemala City?"

I nod.

"He took the photographs that were with the letter, he explains. Some of them were related to the United Fruit Company."

"Yeah, that's an American banana company." I want to tell her more about it, about how they convinced Eisenhower and his people to overthrow the Guatemalan government, but I don't. I'm here just for her to translate.

"He says he was allowed to photograph their workers and property until he wrote a negative story about the company. This next part is very interesting. He talks about a disinformation campaign that the CIA started in Guatemala with a fake radio announcement, supposedly broadcast from a secret location, but actually prerecorded by an actor in Florida. The CIA used the recording to spread lies about President Árbenz and his supporters, to turn people against them. Your great-grandfather calls it psychological warfare."

I feel like I should be taking notes, but I'm too absorbed to get out a pen and paper.

She scans the rest of the page before continuing. "He says

the CIA sent airplanes to intimidate the Guatemalans and make Castillo Armas's forces seem larger. President Árbenz's supporters believed the attackers were more powerful than they really were, making it possible for the coup to succeed."

She turns the paper over. There are only a couple of lines of writing on the back. "He says that he left Guatemala in 1954. He was worried for his life and went to Mexico. And then he has a postscript at the bottom. It says, *I hope this information helps with your research, dear Viviana, and answers some of your questions.*" She folds the letter and hands it back to me.

I imagine my mom wondering about Eugenio the same way I do—wanting to know what was behind the guarded expression in his eyes. Wanting to understand what had happened to him. "Thank you so much. There's no way I would've been able to understand all that."

"Anytime, Sarah. You know, this is some very interesting history. I know a little history about many Spanish-speaking countries, but I don't think I've ever heard this much detail about the coup against the president of Guatemala."

"Yeah, I'm finding out a lot. I'm researching this for an art project. I want to do sketches based on some of my great-grandfather's photographs."

"That sounds amazing. I can't wait to see your project at the art showcase."

"Oh, you know about the showcase?"

"Ms. Escamilla has been doing it for years now. It's a big draw for the community. She usually gets a turnout of a couple hundred people."

A couple hundred! I guess that shouldn't be surprising given the size of the student body alone. But I hadn't been picturing such a major event.

"Let me know how the project goes and if you need help with anything else."

I've heard those words so many times: *let me know if you need anything.* How many people came by our house after my mom died and repeated that to us? Most of them I haven't seen since. I've come to think of the line as an empty recitation, one that fulfills a social obligation but does nothing to actually help anybody. With Señora Dominguez, though, maybe it's different. I stand up and push the chair in. "I will. Thank you."

When I get home, Dad and Steven are making pancakes.

"Breakfast for dinner!" Steven announces, tugging at the straps of one of Mom's old aprons that he's wearing. Dad, who's wearing his own apron, gives me a small smile.

"Sounds yummy." I put my backpack down on one of the kitchen chairs.

"Mom loves hers with blueberries." Steven kneels down in front of the freezer, pulling out a bag of frozen corn, a package of frozen burritos, and two nearly-finished tubs of ice cream. He takes out a little plastic tub of blueberries from the back, and I'm tempted to warn him that they're super old. The freezer has kept them preserved, I hope.

"How do you want yours, Sarah?" Dad asks.

"Hmm, banana nut?"

"You want to slice some bananas for Sarah?" Dad asks Steven.

Steven's eyes dart to the knife block on the counter. "Okay, but I'm not using the Cutco knife. Remember two years ago in November when Mom sliced her finger with the big Cutco knife? She almost had to get stitches. She made me promise to never use that one."

Dad looks at Steven for a moment before he speaks. "I had forgotten about that. You can use a less sharp knife, maybe even a butter knife. Bananas are soft and easy to cut."

Steven pulls out a butter knife followed by a meat tenderizer. "Mom always puts the walnuts in a plastic baggie and then hits it with this thing to break them up." Steven slices the banana on the cutting board and proceeds to hammer the baggie of walnuts with so much force that they're practically crumbs.

I set the table while they finish. Dad and I eat the banana walnut pancakes, while Steven has chocolate chip. The blueberry pancakes go untouched.

"These are great, guys," I say. "Thanks."

"They just need a little of this." Steven takes a can of whipped cream and sprays it in a circular motion all over his pancake.

"Steven, that's probably enough." Dad takes the can from him.

"I know. I know. Mom says don't eat too much sugar." He forks the pancake and takes a huge bite without even attempting to cut it.

"How was your day, Sarah?" Dad asks.

I try to remember the last time he asked such a question. "It was good. I found a letter from Eugenio with those photographs you mentioned. My Spanish teacher translated it for me."

"I remember that letter. The one that talks about the psychological warfare in the fifties?"

I finish a bite of walnut crumbs. "You've read it?"

"A long time ago. Back when your mom was working on a research paper for grad school."

"What is psychological warfare?" Steven asks, his mouth full of pancakes and whipped cream.

"Our great-grandpa wrote this letter describing how the US wanted to overthrow the president of Guatemala, so the CIA—"

"Central Intelligence Agency. I know what that is." Steven forks a second pancake and stuffs his mouth.

I nod. "Yeah, they recorded a fake radio show to turn the Guatemalan people against the president. They made up lies about him and gave money to the guy who wanted to overthrow him. And then they sent these planes to scare everyone into thinking that guy's attack was going to be worse than it actually was. They scared the people so they wouldn't fight."

Dad cuts his pancake. "Some of that radio broadcast is online. We can listen to it sometime if you want."

"The fake broadcast from 1954? Yeah, I'd like to listen to it, but I probably won't understand it."

"We can figure it out together."

Even though she's not here to dive into the pancakes that would always inevitably leave her lips blue, I feel Mom's spirit. I feel it in Dad's small desire to help me with my project and in Steven's enthusiasm over helping in the kitchen. I hope we can hold on to her beyond this moment.

CHAPTER TWENTY-ONE

S teven microwaves four hot dogs and stacks them on a cookie sheet. He piles a bag of chips, two cans of Coke, a bag of Skittles, and a can of peanuts around the hot dogs. Before he leaves the kitchen with his Game Seven snacks, I stop him.

"Listen, Steven. David and I are going to this birthday party. Are you sure you and Dad will be okay?"

"Yes, I already told you, Sarah. We're going to watch the game." His thin limbs vibrate with impatience.

"Okay, but bring your phone into Dad's room. Call me for any reason. And make sure to respond to my texts, okay?"

"Okay, Sarah. I already said yes." He carefully balances the cookie sheet as he heads upstairs. I already had a talk with Dad earlier. I told him where David and I would be and said he could call me if he needed me to come home. He's been doing so well lately. I want to give him this chance to show that he's getting better, that he can be our dad again. Maybe soon he'll even be able to get back to work and we can all start to live more normal lives.

I head upstairs to get ready for my date, pushing away memories of the last time I did this. I don't feel the nervousness from that day. Being with David is so easy when I can focus on just him, on just us, and not be overwhelmed with worries about Dad and Steven. There are no insecurities about whether he likes me enough; there are only feelings of rightness and happiness.

I put on light pink jeans and a white V-neck with thin stripes. I decide to leave my purse here so I don't have to be taking care of it while golfing. I pull out my debit card and ID and put them in my back pocket with my phone. I touch up my makeup and put curl cream into my hair to give my curls definition.

When David arrives, he gives me a soft, short kiss and we head out.

"So how long have you and Bobby been friends?" I ask him.

"Since third grade."

"What were you and little Bobby like in third grade?"

David tosses his head back and laughs. "We hung out almost every day after school. He'd ride his bike to my house; I'd ride my bike to his house. We'd play ball in the street every day. Mostly basketball, sometimes just catch football. We did Little League together. He was good at every sport he tried. He'd win MVP of everything."

I start to get nervous about meeting him, really meeting him. I met him at the fall festival at school when he gave Steven the popcorn, but he didn't know me then. Now, he knows I'm dating David. Am I going to be good enough for this MVP's oldest friend?

Music is blaring from outside speakers as we pull into the very full parking lot of Top Golf. We go inside to the section that Bobby's parents have rented out. There are huge TV screens surrounding the area, showing Game Seven of the World Series.

Bobby comes over and gives David a big hug. He keeps his arm around David as David introduces us.

"Thanks for coming, Sarah. I'm glad we finally get to hang out. I want to get to know this girl David won't stop talking about. It's like Sarah this, Sarah that."

I smile, pretending it's amusing, but deep down, I wonder what David is saying about me. What has he told Bobby?

"Cool tattoo you did on my boy, by the way. He says you're a really good artist."

"Thanks. And he says you were MVP of every sport you tried."

Bobby laughs. "At least we know he tells the truth, right?"

"Roberto!" someone calls behind him. "Mira, aquí está tu tía."

Bobby turns around. "Gotta go say hi to my aunt. Thanks for coming, guys. Hope you have fun."

"He seems really nice," I say to David.

He takes my hand and leads me toward the golf club rental. "Yeah. He's good people. He really wanted to meet you since . . . I guess you're my girlfriend. Are you my girlfriend?" There's a rare waver in his smile. I guess David does get nervous, but this is the first time he's been unable to cover it up with his usual coolness.

I let his hand go and put my arms around his waist, pulling him toward me. "Yes, I'm your girlfriend. I think I pretty much have the MVP of boyfriends."

He kisses my cheek and squeezes me. "You ready to play golf?"

I nod and he leads me to the counter, where we get a bucket of balls and two clubs. We find one of the many tees Bobby's parents have paid for. Golf, sports in general, will never be my thing, but standing here with a club in my hand watching David adjust his stance for a full thirty seconds and take half a dozen practice swings is something I could get used to. I love watching him. I think about how he led the whole fourth grade of Las Positas Elementary in exercise and games. I love how his body moves, the ease with which each of his muscles responds to his will.

He swings and launches the ball well into the air. "You're next."

I take his place at the tee. I put no effort into my stance and take exactly zero practice swings. I do hit the ball, but it only goes about half the length of David's. He kisses me as we switch places. We finish the bucket of balls and go find empty spaces at the food table. I glance at the giant screen. It's the bottom of the third inning, and the Astros are winning. I figure Dad and Steven are glued to the TV.

I slide in next to a girl who I saw holding Bobby's hand earlier. She turns to me and smiles.

"Hi, you're Sarah, right?" She has long brown hair and amazing eyelashes. "I'm Jimena, Bobby's girlfriend." I see her name displayed in cursive on a gold chain she wears around her neck.

I tell her it's nice to meet her. We grab slices of pizza from the center of the table, and David pours root beer from a pitcher into two plastic cups and gives me one.

Jimena holds out her cup for him to fill. "David is cool, Sarah. Good choice. And maybe now he'll finally stop third-wheeling it with us all the time, so I can have my man to myself."

David laughs so hard he can barely chew his pizza.

Jimena smiles at me. "He knows I'm kidding. Maybe we can all go on a double date sometime. What do you think?"

"Yeah, that sounds like fun. What do you and Bobby like to do?"

"We go to the movies a lot. We hang out at his house a lot. His dad likes to grill. We're there almost every Sunday night. We gotta watch our Cowboys most Sundays. But we do outdoors stuff too. Bobby and I like to find new bike trails. We just throw our bikes in his truck and look for a new trail. You and David should come sometime. We can show you our favorite spots."

"I'd like that," I say, and I mean it. Jimena and Bobby seem very nice, nothing like Brad or Brittany. I haven't seen David hanging out with either of those two lately. The fact that he's still close to Bobby after all this time tells me that Bobby's a friend worth having.

We eat our pizza and talk. Jimena tells me some of the ridiculous things David and Bobby have done. Bobby eventually joins us when he's able to extricate himself from his tías and tíos. It feels good, just talking about nothing, about everything. I think back to freshman year at PFA when I sat in the dorm cafeteria in large groups like this, without the heavy worries that now infiltrate almost every thought I have.

Bobby's dad brings over a three-tiered cake and sets it in front of Bobby. Jimena holds up her phone and records everyone singing "Happy Birthday." Bobby beams at his girlfriend the entire time until he blows the candles out.

We stay as Bobby opens his presents. I don't think I've ever seen so many presents at a birthday party that wasn't for a nine-year-old. But Bobby has a lot of friends. He also has many tías and tíos who are very liberal with their twenty-dollar bills. It ends up being a really nice night. And it has probably been a good night for Steven. It's now the ninth inning and the Astros are about to win.

Pretty much everyone at the party is now staring at a screen, as only two more outs will decide the winner of the World

Series. I feel like I should get home soon just to make sure Dad and Steven don't get into any trouble once the game is over.

"Is it okay if we go?" I ask David, who has his arm around me.

"The game's almost done. Is it okay if we stay until it's finished?"

"I think I should check on my dad and Steven. I'm just starting to get worried."

David's face turns serious for the first time all day. I hate that I'm the cause of that. "Yeah, of course. Let's go."

On the way to the car, I keep my fingers interlaced with his. "I had a lot of fun tonight. Thanks for inviting me. I really like Bobby and Jimena."

"Yeah, they're cool. They make a really good couple. It would be fun to double sometime with them."

"Yeah, that would be fun."

In the car, he turns on the car radio, and we listen as the announcers finish calling the game. The Astros have won the World Series, and I expect to get home to an elated Steven and hopefully a content Dad. It's hard to tell how anything will affect Dad these days. Will he be happy that his team won or will he feel melancholy that Mom isn't here to share the moment with him?

David moves one hand off the steering wheel and squeezes my hand. I take his hand in both of mine and hold it on my lap. Maybe I'll invite him over for dinner tomorrow. It seems like such a normal boyfriend/girlfriend thing to do. Invite your boyfriend to dinner. But Dad's behavior still isn't reliable enough for me to slide into a comfortable and normal teenage life. His interactions with David have been so erratic, and I don't want to risk another disaster.

David pulls into my driveway. David pulls into my driveway.

156

DAVID PULLS INTO MY DRIVEWAY.

He shouldn't be able to pull into my driveway because I park my car in the center of it every day. But my car isn't there.

Déjà vu comes barreling at me. I can't handle this again. I yank the car door open without saying anything and run toward the house.

David is right behind me. "Sarah, are you okay?"

I open the front door, letting it slam against the wall. "Steven! Dad!"

"Sarah." David comes in behind me, alarm running through his eyes.

"My car's not here. Steven!"

There's no answer, and there's nobody downstairs. The house is silent. I lunge up the stairs. In my dad's room, the television is on, but he isn't there. I clutch the railing and force myself downstairs on unsteady feet.

I'm on my way out the back door to check the backyard when I stop suddenly in the dining room. My purse is spilled open on the dining room table. It's turned on its side, the contents splayed across the table. My sunglasses case is there with some old receipts and my hand cream, but my keys and wallet are missing.

I drop to my knees and scramble around on the floor, looking under the dining table, hoping my keys are there somewhere. But no. My keys, my wallet, my car, my father, and my brother are all gone.

David puts a hand on my shoulder. "No luck?"

I stagger to my feet only to collapse into his waiting arms. He rubs his hand up and down my back.

"What if something happened?" I whimper. *Not now*, I silently instruct my tears. *Stop crying now.* He shouldn't have to deal with this kind of weakness, this kind of neediness from me.

"We'll find them. Where should we start looking?"

Vic. I have to call Vic. "Hang on. We have a friend who can help." I walk away from David and dial Vic's number.

He answers right away. "Sarah, is everything okay?" He knows I don't call him. I always text him.

Vic's worried voice releases something within me. I let go of the tears I've been holding back, of the panic I've been trying to suppress.

I start sobbing so hard that I can hardly get the words out. "They're gone. They're both gone. My car is gone. I don't know where they went."

"Okay, I'm coming. Did you try calling them?"

"No, not yet."

"Okay, I'll call Paul. You call Steven," Vic says. "I'm on my way."

Of course. Call Steven. Come on, Sarah. Quit falling apart and think.

No answer. I text him, but nothing. Steven sucks at texting. He doesn't even like having a phone. I make him keep it with him just in case, exactly for moments like this. He loses his phone half the time, and I have to help him find it.

He loses his phone! I remember we installed a find-a-phone app on it after the last time he misplaced it. We eventually found it under his bed.

I open my app and see that Steven's phone is at a drive-in burger place we go to sometimes.

"I think he's at Sonic," I say to David.

"Let's go."

David drives while I text Vic and send him Steven's location.

It's less than two miles away, but the drive there feels like a torturous eternity. We pull up to the front of the restaurant, but we don't see my car. David drives around to the back, and there, illuminated under a tall post, is my Toyota—one tire up on the curb, its back bumper smashed against the lamppost. Steven and my dad are sitting in the front. David stops his Jeep, and we both rush over.

"Steven!" I run to the passenger side and bend down.

He's crying; his hands are covering his face.

"Steven, are you okay?"

Still covering his eyes, Steven turns to me, shakes his head, and buries his face in my shoulder. I pull him out of the car and put my arms around him, squeezing him to me. I look at my dad behind the steering wheel. David is standing by the driver's side door, his hand hovering over the handle, not knowing what to do.

"Sarah, I'm so sorry. I'm so sorry. I'm so sorry, Steven." My dad looks to me, to Steven, and back. "We were about to go home, and then all of the sudden the car starts going in reverse. It just goes in reverse."

I want to yell at him, to ask him why he took my car in the first place, but my voice won't work. I look around the parking lot to see if people are watching, but it's sparse. This is the back of Sonic, and most cars park in the front. The buildings back here are mostly small businesses and offices that are closed at this time of night. It's past eleven, so it's mostly quiet and very dark.

Screeching tires come to a halt just behind David's Jeep. It's Vic. He sprints over to me. "Are they okay?"

"Yeah, they're fine." I run my hand up and down Steven's back.

Vic circles around the car to the driver's side to speak to

Dad just as David moves aside and joins Steven and me. To my relief, David doesn't say anything.

Vic speaks to Dad, but I can't hear what he's saying. Dad gets out of the car and comes over to us.

"I'm sorry, Steven. I'm sorry, Sarah. I . . . I . . . I don't know what happened."

Vic puts his hand on my dad's shoulder. "Let's get you home. Okay?" He looks at me. "Sarah, we need to get your dad out of here. Somebody could come by here, see the car, call the police."

I look over at my dad. He's been drinking. He's drunk. He could be arrested for driving drunk with a child in the car.

Vic walks over to his truck and comes back with a tow strap. He says to David, "Will you strap this to Sarah's car? I'm going to back up into it and pull the car off the curb. Paul said the wheel won't go over the curb."

I pull Steven back, and we watch as Vic slowly pulls my car over the curb. It doesn't take long, and he works fast to put away the tow strap in his truck.

"I'm going to take Paul home. Sarah, I think your car is still drivable. Why don't you and Steven take it home? Pull it into the garage if you can. We don't need your neighbors asking questions. We'll be right behind you."

I put Steven in the car and turn to David. "Thank you. I'll talk to you tomorrow."

He takes a step toward me. "Can I come over and make sure everything is okay?"

I put a hand out to distance him from me. I can't talk to him right now. "No. Thank you, but I think we need it to be just us tonight."

"Will you call me later?"

I nod, but I'm not sure that I will.

The car makes a terrible sound all the way home. Steven has his knees pulled up to his chest, and his arms are wrapped around his skinny legs.

"Why did you go with him, Steven? Why didn't you call me?"

"He said we were going to get milkshakes to celebrate the Astros. He said we'd be quick. He said we'd be right back."

I know it's not Steven's fault. He put his trust in Dad tonight, as any eight-year-old should be able to do with their father. "You should never get in the car with him, Steven."

"But I've always gone places with him. He's always taken me places. I don't get it."

He shouldn't have to get it. He shouldn't have to be responsible for keeping himself safe around his own father. But I can't shield him from reality anymore. "Dad isn't the same person who took you to school every day, who took you to football and baseball games, who took you to get ice cream. He's not able to make safe choices anymore. You can never go with him in the car again. Never, Steven." I hear the clunk of metal coming from the rear of the car.

"Okay, Sarah. Okay."

We pull into the driveway and I move stuff over in the garage to make room for my Toyota. After I've parked it, I get a good look at the bumper for the first time tonight. It's bent right in the middle. I'm not sure how I was able to get it home.

We go into the kitchen through the garage door. Vic has taken my dad upstairs. I don't even want to be anywhere near Dad.

At the bottom of the stairs I say to Steven, "I was thinking maybe you could sleep in my bed tonight, and I'll just sleep in my sleeping bag on the floor."

"Why?" Steven asks.

"Well, I just would sleep better knowing you were in the room. It was really scary coming home to find you missing."

Steven shrugs and climbs up the stairs. He goes into his room to change while I strip my bed and put on clean sheets. I throw the dirty sheets into a corner and pull my sleeping bag out of my closet.

Vic stops in my doorway on his way to the stairs. "Hey, Sarah. Got him settled."

"Thank you so much for your help, Vic. I don't know what I would've done without you."

Vic slides a hand over his face. It's been a tough night for him too. Friendship with my dad has come with some heavy lifting, and I wonder if he regrets it.

"I'm just glad nothing worse happened. And I'm glad you called me. Paul's in a bad place right now. He said the night started out good, watching the game with Steven. And then he just started missing your mom so much, and he kept drinking. Next thing you know, they're going for milkshakes and he backs up into that post."

"*I* miss my mom, but I don't do stuff like this."

"I know, Sarah. And he feels terrible. He says he really wants help this time. I don't have class in the morning, so I'm going to come by, and we're going to call that therapist to make an appointment. He says he's ready."

I shake my head, not sure I believe that even this will make a difference.

"And when I come in the morning, I'll call a few places to see where we can take your car to get it fixed. You won't be able to file a claim with the insurance. They'll ask too many questions."

There's no way I'll be able to get it fixed, then. I don't have enough money; it's sure to cost thousands of dollars. "Can't I just put it through the insurance and tell them I was driving?"

"That's up to you. I just don't want you to get in trouble. Can you get a ride to school with your, uh, friend?"

I think about David. He wanted to come home with me tonight to make sure we were okay. I pushed him away. I don't want to talk to him right now; I don't know what I would say to him. "Actually, can you give me a ride?"

"Sure. What time does school start for you?"

"Nine."

"Got it. Call me if you need anything before that."

"Thanks for everything, Vic."

A minute later Steven comes into my room wearing his pajamas. "I brushed my teeth." He climbs on my bed and starts jumping on it. "I love your bed. Thanks for letting me sleep on it."

"Sure. I was also thinking maybe we should stay home from school tomorrow.

Steven sits up in bed. "Why?"

"It's been a rough night. Maybe we just take a day?"

"No, Sarah. Me and Ryan and basically our whole lunch table are having a celebration lunch. We said if the Astros win, we have a party at lunch. And I'm supposed to bring the Pixy Stix."

"Are you sure you're okay to go to school?" Honestly, I'm hoping he'll say no, if only so I have an excuse to stay home with him. That way I won't have to make Vic give me a ride—I can text him to let him know he's off the hook.

"Yes, I'm sure," Steven insists. "And when can we go get the Pixy Stix?"

"Steven, it's after midnight."

"Well, Dad was going to take me after the milkshakes."

"Can you take something else? There's a box of fruit snacks in the pantry. Why don't you just take those?"

"Fine." Steven turns his back to me and pulls the covers over his shoulder. In a smaller voice, he adds, "Good night, Sarah."

"Good night." I place my sleeping bag in front of the door and do something I've never done. I turn the lock on my door, for the first time in my life.

It's been a long night; it almost feels like one night ran into the next one. I don't even know what time it is, and I'm too tired to find my phone. I know that David has probably texted, but I don't have the energy to talk to him right now.

Steven's long legs are sprawled on my bed in the dim moonlight that filters into my room. Something could have happened to him tonight, something worse than the small accident. I've already lost my mother. My father is unreachable. I can't lose Steven. I lean against the door and close my eyes.

CHAPTER TWENTY-TWO

Across the room, my phone alarm blares, and I hop out of my sleeping bag to grab it. Steven sits up in my bed and stretches his arms over his head. "Your bed is so comfortable. Can I sleep here every night?"

I smile at him. It's so good to see he's woken up in a good mood. I seriously consider making this our new routine so I can know he's safe. "Why don't you go get ready for school, and I'll walk you to the bus?"

While Steven's getting dressed, I conquer all my instincts and walk to Dad's room. He sits in his recliner in the corner. It looks like he's just showered. His wet hair is combed back, and he's dressed with his shoes on like he's about to go somewhere.

When he sees me, the weeping starts in the pit of his stomach and reaches his throat, where it comes out in long, breathless sobs. His body shakes.

"I'm sorry," he says.

"I don't care. It's not enough to say you're sorry. You've ruined your life and now you're ruining ours."

The sobbing continues. I don't want to be cruel, but something needs to shake him off the road to self-destruction.

"You are the grown-up. He is the child, and he is the one suffering because of you." I walk toward him, hoping my words will resonate with him, will make him realize that he needs to do more than endlessly apologize.

I open his closet and pull out a cardboard box that holds rolls of toilet paper. I turn the box over and dump out the remaining rolls. Some end up out in the hallway.

I walk to the recliner, pick up the almost-full bottle he was sucking on yesterday, and fling it into the empty box. I find two unopened bottles under his bed. Cheap whiskey—the luxury of Johnnie Walker Gold forgotten. I add these bottles to my collection. They clank against each other but don't break. If they had broken, it wouldn't have mattered. My mission is to destroy, not to preserve.

"What are you doing?" Dad asks.

"It's all going. Every one of these!" I snatch a bottle off the top of his bureau.

He covers his face with his hands.

I open each of the drawers looking for a secret stash. One of the drawers comes right out of the bureau as I pull it with one hand and unknown strength. I let it fall to the ground with a thump. "You are done. No more! She's gone! She's never coming back."

His sobs intensify, and I have to look away. "I'm sorry, Dad." I sink onto his newly made bed.

He's hunched over now, his face in his hands. "You're right. I know you are. Vic's going to take me to get help. I promise, Sarah. I am going to do better. I know I have to."

I look up at him, wondering if for once he really means it. His head is still in his hands. "Last night was really scary," he goes on. "The accident could've been worse. I could've hurt Steven. I could've hurt someone else, maybe been arrested."

"You could be dead. And Stephen and I would have no one."

This realization shakes me. Yesterday, all my thoughts were about Steven and his well-being. Today, it finally dawns on me that I could have lost my dad. I start crying, letting out all the tears I pushed aside last night.

He comes over to sit beside me, his hands clasped between his legs. I put my head on his shoulder, and he brings his arms around me.

"I'm so sorry, Sarah. I promise; I'm going to get better and do better."

I run my hand across Mom's quilt and wish for the millionth time that she was here. "Okay" is all I can say to him.

We sit there for a few more minutes before I pull myself off his bed. "I'm going to take Steven to the bus, and then Vic is taking me to school."

He acknowledges this with a nod, and I leave without saying goodbye.

Vic tells me it's a good sign that Dad showered, got dressed, and was waiting for him. It shows that he followed through on what he told Vic last night. After he drops me off, Vic will go back to our house to help Dad make his first therapy appointment. I thank him for everything and tell him I'll find a ride home.

David is waiting for me outside physics class. I've ignored a dozen texts and two phone calls from him between last night and this morning.

"I'm sorry I didn't text you back. There was a lot going on," I say to him.

He reaches for my hand. "That's okay. Is everyone all right?"

I nod. I watch as students filter into the classroom, and I try to keep my voice down. "Yeah, Steven is okay. He went to school. And Vic is going to help my dad get an appointment with a therapist."

"That's good. I was really worried about you, though."

I just want to go to class and start the day. I don't want to have this conversation with him right here, right now. "I know. And it was kind of awful of me not to respond, but I was dealing with worrying about two other people. I don't have it in me to worry about three right now."

"Hey. I'm not trying to make you feel guilty. I just want you to know that I care about you."

"David, I told you before. I already tried to explain this."

"What?"

"I can't do this. Yesterday with you was nice. It was normal. But normal is not my life. It's so complicated right now. I'm responsible for two people besides myself. Every time I've let my guard down, look what's happened." Tears threaten to emerge, and I have to clamp my mouth shut to keep everything in.

"That's not fair. What happened wasn't your fault. Us spending time together is not the problem."

The hallway has emptied out; first period is about to start. "I know that. I know my dad is responsible for what happened, but I'm the one who has to deal with it." I point to my chest for emphasis. "I'm the one who has to make sure my brother is safe and my dad doesn't end up dead or in jail."

I can't listen to his response. I can't have one more person's happiness hinge on me. I walk into class and leave him behind.

David follows and sits across from me, but I look up at Mr. Lemmon and try to focus on what he's saying. When he can't get my attention, David sends me a text.

DAVID: Can we talk? Please.

I wait until after class is done, and we walk out together.

"Let's go outside," I say, second period forgotten.

We walk in silence to the front of the school, out the main doors and around the side of the building, where we can't be seen through the office windows. We stand behind a full row of yellow bells. The blooms are withering, and the seed pods weigh the thin stems down to the ground. Someone had good intentions when they planted these, but their minimal upkeep makes them a sorry sight right now.

David leans against the brick wall, facing me, and lightly touches my fingertips. "Sarah, I'm not trying to make things harder for you."

I pull my hand out of his loose grasp. "I know you're not trying to, but all your texts and calls and wanting to talk right now—that's only making things harder for me."

He sighs and straightens up. "I was just so worried about you when you didn't respond. I almost drove back to your house. I didn't know if something had happened, if your dad—"

"My dad isn't a mean drunk. He wouldn't do anything to hurt me on purpose."

"I . . . I just didn't know since you didn't reply to my texts."

"I get that. But that's why I just don't think we should do the boyfriend/girlfriend thing anymore. You have certain expectations as my boyfriend." It seems cruel, but I say the word *boyfriend* with air quotes. "And I can't handle your expectations right now."

"Texting back that you're okay? It's not like that's a huge obligation. It takes like two seconds."

"It's not just two seconds. There would've been follow-up

texts, and I just couldn't deal with that. I could've lost my little brother last night, and texting you back was not the priority."

I've never seen his eyes like this. All the light dims from them. I have never been the cause of diminishing something so precious before.

He looks down to the ground and swallows hard. "I know what happened last night was terrible and really hard for you, but I only want to support you. I love you, Sarah."

"Well, I can't deal with your love right now."

I leave him there, standing behind the withering yellow bells. I run back inside the school and find a bathroom where I can hide.

CHAPTER TWENTY-THREE

Makaila gives me a ride home; I've told her I had car trouble. For the first few minutes of the drive we talk about school, especially COOP, since Makaila is presenting on Wednesday. "Your lesson day is coming up too," she says to me. "What did you decide to teach the kids?"

"Well, I'm still not sure . . ."

"Sarah, it's this Friday!"

"I know. I know. I've been so focused on the art show that I'm having a hard time figuring this out." Not that I've made much progress with my art project either. My second meeting with Ms. Escamilla is tomorrow, and I have no real updates for her.

"Let me know if you want help brainstorming or putting stuff together," says Makaila.

"Thanks. I'll try to come up with a lesson plan tonight and go from there."

She pulls into my driveway. "I'm happy to give you a ride, but is everything okay with David? Y'all seemed off today in class."

In COOP today, David sat in the corner, slumped back, his head lowered onto his hand, his usual bright energy extinguished.

I take off my seat belt but stay seated. "Yeah. I broke up with him. It just isn't a good time for a relationship right now.

Things are complicated at home." I pause. I haven't told many people more than that, but I feel like I can trust Makaila. "Ever since my mom died, it's been really hard for us, and my family really needs me and I can't make time for David like a girlfriend should."

"I'm sorry. David shouldn't put that kind of pressure on you."

"He's been really good, very understanding, but I just can't be his girlfriend right now."

"I'm sorry about your mom and everything. And now your car? That sucks. Need a ride tomorrow?"

"I'm probably going to sign up for the bus. I don't think my car is getting fixed any time soon."

"You cannot take the bus. That's for freshmen and sophomores. I can pick you up."

"Are you sure?"

"Yeah, I'm only like two miles from here. I'll pick you up and bring you home as long as you need."

"Thank you. That would be a big help."

She hugs me before I get out of the car. In the house, Steven is in the living room watching a World Series highlights show on ESPN. Dad sits at the kitchen table with his laptop.

"Hey, Sarah." He looks up at me, taking his reading glasses off.

"Hi. How was today?" I ask, hoping all the promises he made haven't vanished into this morning's fog.

"It was good. Vic helped me make an appointment with a therapist he knows. I'm going on Wednesday. He's going to take me before his last class."

"That's good, Dad. I think it could really help."

He puts his glasses back on and faces the computer screen. "I promise I'm going to do better."

Steven comes in from the living room. "Is the pizza here yet?"

"Pizza?" I ask.

"I ordered pizza. I don't want you to always have to worry about dinner," Dad says.

"He couldn't find anything good to make for dinner, and there's no milk for cereal," Steven adds. "When are you going grocery shopping?"

I shut my eyes. I blew most of last week's grocery budget on the snacks he requested for Game Seven, figuring I'd just have to find a way to stretch out the pantry contents for another few days. "Well, Steven. I don't have any money, and I can't drive my car, so how do you expect me to even get groceries?"

"Okay, okay. Sorry."

I immediately feel guilty for snapping at him.

Dad looks over at me again. "I'm going to set up a weekly grocery delivery," he says. "I can tell we're running out of things. And you shouldn't have to be in charge of that on top of everything else you handle, Sarah."

I can't argue with that, except maybe to ask how he plans to pay for a grocery delivery service. But he's not finished.

"I'm also going to withdraw some funds from my retirement account so we can get your car fixed. Vic's going to help me get an estimate tomorrow."

"Are you sure?"

"Of course. You need your car. I have to get it fixed for you."

I slide into a chair across from him. "Thank you."

"It's Gino's," says Steven. "The pizza. Remember that place, Sarah? Remember when we went there with Mom? She said it tasted just like real New York pizza. She ordered the pepperoni and mushrooms, and I wouldn't eat it because the mushrooms were touching my pepperonis, and Mom ordered me my own pizza." Steven is laughing now at the memory. "I was so picky when I was six." He shakes his head. "But Mom said she was happy to have so many leftovers because Gino's Pizza tasted just like Caruso's Pizza in New York City when she and Dad went there for New Year's Eve when they were in grad school."

I remember that now. It seems like so long ago when we ate at Gino's Pizza, and I'm impressed that Steven remembers that day in so much detail. Dad watches Steven as he goes on and on about that one small moment in our family's history. The doorbell rings, and Steven flies to the front door.

"Thanks for dinner," I say to Dad. "I'll come back in a few minutes and grab a slice."

I take my backpack into the office. Out of the corner of my eye I see Dad get up, push his laptop aside, and grab some plates.

I sit cross-legged on the love seat and pull my backpack up next to me. I've been carrying my great-grandpa Eugenio's pictures with me every day, hoping they'll inspire me. I go through each picture again. The bananas stacked beside the train cars. The workers next to the bananas. The people holding up the "Viva Árbenz" sign. The men holding rifles. The troops on the truck.

It wasn't that long ago that David was in here with me, helping me find these pictures. My search was his search. He was committed to my personal mission. I can't be there for him in any way, and that's why I had to break up with him. I can't return the love and support he's offered me, so I shouldn't be with him.

I pull my Sharpies out of my backpack and pick the Jupiter-red one. I find a spot on my bicep that can be easily covered up by most of my shirts. After I've prepped the area, I start drawing a large heart. I fill it in with bold color.

David's love for me is genuine and generous. It's a real kind of love that I've never had before, and I don't know when or even if I'll find something like it again. It's crushing that I had to walk away from that. It isn't fair to him, but it is also not fair to me. It wasn't a decision I wanted to make; it was a decision I *had* to make. Maybe someday I'll see it differently, see it as a mistake, but for now, I have to be here in this house making sure that the two out there eating pizza stay alive and safe.

I finish my heart tattoo. I will wear it around, for only me to see, knowing that it represents a beautiful love I briefly shared with a kind boy whose gorgeous eyes are the color of honey.

I pull my sleeve down. I'll look at it when I need to be reminded of that love. Right now, I'm going to focus on my mom, on her family, and on telling this story.

Mom's filing cabinet and bookcase are full of information, and I don't know where to start. I'm drawn to the biographies on her bottom bookshelf. She has several books about Diego Rivera, the artist she loved so much that she used most of her wall space to feature his art. One has a picture of Frida Kahlo, another Mexican artist, on the cover, and I wonder why. When I start reading this book, I find out that Diego Rivera and Frida Kahlo were married. I've heard of Frida Kahlo; I think pretty much everyone has. Her eyebrows are legendary, and her image is found in so many places—on T-shirts, handbags, pillows, posters, notebooks. She's become commercialized, and I wonder what she would think of that.

As I continue to read, I learn she was an activist and used her art to make political statements. On a hunch, I thumb through Mom's file cabinet and find a thick manila folder labeled *Frida*.

In the file is a collection of articles and pictures. One piece that I skim talks about Frida attending a protest against US intervention in Guatemala. I want to read more about this. Why was it so important to her? Why was it so important to her husband, Diego Rivera? They were both Mexican, not Guatemalan. Yet an event in a neighboring country that didn't affect them mattered enough to them that she protested it publicly and he painted a mural about it.

Frida was very sick during the last few years of her life, was confined to a wheelchair, had her leg amputated at the knee, and still she protested in Mexico when the US overthrew Árbenz in Guatemala. She died a few days after her protest. It seems unbelievable to me that as she was dying, she chose to show up in support of the Guatemalan people. Maybe that's what inspired Rivera to paint *Gloriosa Victoria*.

The last item in the file folder is a printout of an online petition to rename the Dulles International Airport. The tracking bar along the side of the page shows that Mom signed the petition about a year ago, and at the time it had fewer than a hundred signatures.

Dad comes in with two slices of pizza on a plate. "I thought you might be hungry."

I take the plate from him and show him the petition. "Mom signed this petition to rename the Dulles Airport?"

"Oh, yeah. I remember she mentioned something about it, but it never took off. I don't think they got enough signatures to be taken seriously."

"It *should* be renamed." I take a bite out of the first slice. "Mmm. This is so good."

"Are you looking for more ideas for your art project?"

"Yeah. I've been reading through a lot of Mom's stuff. This Frida Kahlo connection to Guatemala is so interesting. Frida Kahlo is like this pop culture icon, but I had no idea how politically active she was." She's so iconic even elementary school kids have seen her image. The thought evolves in my mind: what if I make my Las Positas art lesson about Frida?

"Was the photo album any help?" Dad asks before I can get too caught up in this new idea.

"Oh, yes! Actually, I think I want to draw my own versions of these photographs for the art show." I dig Eugenio's photos out of my backpack and show him.

"Wow. I haven't actually looked at these in a long time. Eugenio really had an insider's view of what was going on."

"That's why I want to tell the story of the coup from his perspective. But I still need to do a lot of research for the presentation that'll go with the artwork. Will you help me? I'm sure I'll have so many questions."

He nods. "Yeah. Right now?"

"No, I need to work on another school assignment tonight. But maybe this weekend?"

"Sure, this weekend. You'll need some good online sources to go along with your mom's notes. Tomorrow I'll try to find some reputable websites you can use."

"Okay, thanks, Dad."

"And I want you to keep in mind—not everyone wants to see the US being criticized for past actions. Not everyone in your audience will agree with you."

"How can they not agree that what the US did was bad?"

"Some people won't see it that way. I just want you to know that going into this. But I'll be there and I will support you all the way through."

I wonder if I can actually count on his support. At least he's offering. This is the first time in a long time that he's seemed focused on me at all. "Thanks, Dad."

He smiles a small, brief smile before leaving the office. I thumb through one of Mom's Frida Kahlo books while I finish the pizza. There's a photograph of Frida with Diego Rivera at the protest against the coup. It's the last photograph ever taken of her. Eleven days later, she would die.

She's holding a sign with a dove that reads "Por la Paz." I do a Google Translate for the Spanish phrase. It means *for peace*.

I pick up the petition to rename Dulles International Airport. This was my mom's way of protesting the same atrocity that Frida Kahlo protested. Dad said it hadn't received enough signatures. I go online to see that the petition is still active but hasn't seen a new signature in more than six months. It would need just a couple hundred more signatures to reach its goal. I don't know exactly what would happen after that, but I sign the petition, bookmark the link, and print out a page with two columns of blank lines for more signatures.

I tuck the signature page into my school binder to show Ms. Escamilla tomorrow. I can't just tell the story of the 1954 CIA coup against the Guatemalan president. I have to do more. I have to follow my art with action. It's what Frida would've done; it's what my mom wanted to do; it's what I must do.

CHAPTER TWENTY-FOUR

First-period physics is the last place I want to be. Seeing David's tortured posture and the absence of his usual exuberance is unsettling. I rub the Sharpie heart on my arm, wishing it was his hand I could touch instead of this empty token that only signifies loss.

He doesn't once look over at me. He opens his notebook, taking the notes that Mr. Lemmon projects on a screen. I try to take notes too, but all I want to do is walk over to him, peer over his shoulder, and stare at his messy handwriting.

I caused this change in him. I've hurt him so much and I don't think I'll ever be able to repair it. All he offered was love—unselfish love, something people can go a lifetime without experiencing—and I threw it back in his face.

I still think it was the right thing to do.

I tell Makaila I won't be in COOP today. I hide out in the library behind a shelf of dusty auto mechanic books. I check my email, and there are three messages from my Etsy customers wondering when I'll finish their portraits. I close the email app and shove my phone in my backpack. I don't know how I'll be able to keep up with those customers on top of everything else I already have to do.

When I meet with Ms. Escamilla after school, I show her what I have so far.

She puts her glasses on to get a good look at my completed portrait of Eugenio. "This turned out very well, Sarah. The way you've captured him makes him look like a storyteller, like he's seen a lot that he wants to share with the world. And this second one looks like it's coming along."

"Thank you." That one is of the banana plantation. Stacks of bananas serve as the backdrop for the Guatemalan workers who pose in the foreground. I'm about halfway done with it. The rest of the photos, I've stacked in order of how I will tell the story, ending with a big question mark that I wrote on an index card. The last sketch has to have a big impact, and I feel it should be my own—something that fits with Eugenio's photos but is also separate from them. I'm not sure what that is yet.

"And how are you planning to mount them? Remember that the showcase will be in the school cafeteria, so you'll need to come up with a way to display the pieces."

I hadn't actually remembered that, so I bluff. "I'm still thinking that over. And I know I have to put my speech together too." I pause because I don't know how she's going to receive this next part. "I want to finish up with a petition." I slide the printout across the table to her.

She adjusts her glasses and looks at it.

"It's a petition to rename the Dulles International Airport in Washington, DC," I explain. "It's named after John Foster Dulles, who was the secretary of state when the US overthrew President Árbenz. He did a lot to support the coup. I just don't think someone who's responsible for so much suffering should have an airport named after him. I was thinking that at the end of my speech, I can ask people to sign the petition."

Ms. Escamilla twists her lips. "I think this is an important story you're telling, but I'm not sure that admin will allow you to have a petition. They like to remain politically neutral."

I expected pushback. This is no surprise. "But art has a tradition of being political. Lots of art is meant to inspire us to act. This is a terrible thing that happened in 1954. Democracy in this little country was destroyed. The US supported dictators who killed their people with guns paid for with US dollars. There was a civil war for thirty-six years. Thirty-six years! And the guy who helped start it all got an airport named after him. The least we can do is recognize the injustice of what he did, and fight the idea that we should celebrate terrible people."

Ms. Escamilla takes off her glasses and studies me. "I understand how you feel. And yes, art can be political. I personally have no problem with you asking people to sign a petition. But I have to talk to admin before I can approve it."

I nod, somewhat relieved at this tiny concession. "Okay." I gather my photographs and put everything into my bag.

"Thank you for sharing all of this, Sarah. I admire your desire to speak out about this issue. It shows a lot of courage."

I nod. "Thanks."

As I walk toward the front entrance, the halls have thinned out. Most people are now amassed in the parking lot trying to leave. The sounds of skidding tennis shoes and bouncing balls reverberate as I pass the gym.

Too fast for me to see him coming, David sprints toward the gym entrance. I skid to a stop and so does he; we barely avoid a collision.

Of course. He has basketball practice. He's dressed in those black athletic shorts with the white stripes and a Richards High T-shirt. "Hi."

"Hi," I say and look down at the floor.

"You doing okay?"

I nod. "I just feel really bad about how things ended between us."

"Yeah, me too."

I look up at him to see if the brightness of his eyes has returned. It hasn't. "You must really hate me," I say.

"I don't hate you, Sarah. I love you. But it's really hard knowing that you don't feel the same way."

I do love him. I know that I do. "I hoped we could still be friends."

"I hope we can too, but I think I need some time. Some space."

"It hurts that you won't even look at me in class."

He stares at the gym doors. "It hurts to look at you. I put myself out there, and I tried to show you that you could trust me, and it felt like none of that mattered to you."

His words feel like a stab. "It does matter. I do care. I wish that . . . things could be different." *That I could think only about myself. That I could be with you.*

"Doesn't make this any easier." He's still looking at the gym doors like he wants to escape behind them.

"Okay. I can give you space. I'm really sorry." I get the last word out just before a hard rock drops into my throat.

I rush to the main entrance. The front doors close behind me as my shoulders start shaking and a low, throaty sound forces its way out of my mouth. Two girls sitting on the curb turn to look at me.

Makaila has a student council meeting, so I told her I would wait for her in the parking lot. I hurry to her car, wiping my face with the sleeve of my sweater as I walk. It takes a while for the tears to subside.

I slink down to a crouch beside Makaila's car and text Steven to make sure everything is okay. Since the accident, he's become more responsible about texting me back right away.

Next, I FaceTime Alexa, and seeing my friend makes me start crying all over again. It takes me a minute to compose myself before I can talk.

"Sarah, what is it?"

I haven't talked to her since before the accident. "Everything is screwed up right now. It sucks."

"Are things okay with David?"

I shake my head, and the tears start up again. I tell her about Steven and Dad and about why I had to break up with David.

"Oh, Sarah. It sounds like he really loves you."

I nod. "He does. And I love him too, but I don't think I can tell him that."

"You didn't really want to break up with him?"

I shake my head.

"Well then, be with him."

She says it like it's that easy, but she doesn't see how everything is piling on top of me. "I can't."

"Sarah, I know you have a lot going on, but you don't have to carry it all by yourself. You can lean on somebody else from time to time. You need that. You need love."

"I have love—from you, from my family . . ."

"Yes, that's great, but you deserve this kind of love too. Don't throw it away. Just tell David you need some time to figure everything out."

"I think it's too late for that."

"If he loves you, it's not too late. Give him a few days and then talk to him again. Say that you still care about him and that maybe at some point . . ."

I sigh. "Okay. I'll see. What's new with you, though?"

"Ugh. Drama in the dorms. Drama at dance class. You know. I'll fill you in on all the details when I see you in person over break."

As much as I miss PFA, I don't miss all the drama. "I can't wait to see you."

"Only two and a half more weeks!" We make plans to hang out the day after Thanksgiving, while she's back in San Antonio to see her family, and I feel a little better about everything. Hanging out with Alexa for the first time since the summer will be so good for me. I try not to think about Thanksgiving itself—our first big holiday since Mom's death, our first without her. Maybe if we just pretend it's an ordinary day, we'll all be able to get through it and Dad won't feel compelled to dull his pain with alcohol.

When I get home, Dad and Steven are in the kitchen. Steven is stuffing freshly microwaved frozen meatballs into sub rolls and Dad is spreading sauce over them.

"Meatball subs?" I ask, putting my bag down on the counter.

"Yeah, Sarah. Yours is next. We're making them one at a time." Steven somehow has tomato sauce all over his hands and forearms. He puts mozzarella on top of the first sub and moves on to the next.

"How was your day?" Dad asks me, stirring the bowl of sauce he's holding.

"It was okay." I slide into a chair. I guess I'm off the hook for dinner, so I can sit for a minute. "I talked to my art teacher about my project. I told her I want to bring the airport petition to the art show. After I tell the story of the coup and what Dulles did, I want to ask if people will sign it."

"What's a petition?" Steven asks, tomato sauce dripping from his hands onto the floor.

Dad hands him a paper towel. "It's when people make a statement, usually voicing a belief about an issue or asking for a change of some kind, and then other people sign their names to show that they support that statement—that they believe the same thing or want the same change." Dad explains why Mom supported this particular petition.

"What does a petition have to do with your art class?" Steven asks me as Dad puts the subs in the oven to melt the cheese.

"My project for our art show is about everything that happened in Guatemala, and I want to talk about this issue." I tell him about Frida Kahlo and how she, as an artist, protested the coup.

"Is that the eyebrow lady?" he says.

Dad and I both laugh. The timer goes off, and Dad gets the subs out of the oven. We sit down at the table and dig in. I wonder if this—eating together, talking about our days, even laughing—will become our new normal.

CHAPTER TWENTY-FIVE

Today is a big day. It is the day I will find out if Dad intends to follow through on his promises. Vic is taking Dad to his first therapy appointment this morning. They'll also drop my car off at the repair shop. When I go to check on Dad before I take Steven to the bus stop, I hear the shower running in his bathroom, which is a good sign, so I head downstairs.

Steven sits at the counter waiting for his waffles to emerge from the toaster. He tries to catch them as they pop up. While I eat a yogurt mixed with granola, he drenches his waffles with syrup and shovels them into his mouth.

"Steven, put on a jacket or a hoodie before we leave."

"But it's not even cold."

"It's getting a little bit colder now. Just bring it, okay?"

"Sarah, that's Texas cold. It's not even real cold. Mom says I only have to wear a jacket if it's Boston cold." He grabs a hoodie off the coat hooks by the door and drags it out with him. We walk to the bus stop together, and he runs to meet his friend Ryan, giving me a hurried wave over his shoulder.

Back at the house, Dad is downstairs making a smoothie in the hasn't-been-used-in-almost-a-year blender. I haven't seen Smoothie Dad in so long; it's almost as if he existed in a different lifetime. He puts in a whole banana, some blueberries, and some yogurt. The sound of the blender fills the room, and its harsh noise brightens the morning a bit.

I rinse the lake of syrup off Steven's plate. "What time is your appointment?"

"Nine thirty. Vic will be here in a few minutes." He pours the smoothie into a tall glass and washes the blender in the sink.

"I'm really glad you're going, Dad. I think it's going to make a big difference."

He nods. "I'm going to try. You and Steven deserve better." He takes a step toward me, and I lean in for a hug. His hugs haven't felt genuine for a long time, but this one is like one of the old Dad's hugs.

As I watch Vic's pickup drive away, hope spreads through me. I know one therapy visit won't erase more than six months' worth of pain, won't make him miraculously healthier or more stable right away. But I cling to this little morsel of hope.

Makaila picks me up, and I tell her that my dad is taking my car to get fixed but it might be a few more days before I can drive it again.

"I don't mind, really. It's nice to have someone to walk into school with. Sometimes the size of that place is overwhelming."

"Agreed. My old school had ten percent of the students. This place is huge."

"Oh, wow. Your old school was tiny."

"Yeah, I miss it sometimes."

"Well, I'm glad you're here. You're cool."

I manage to smile. "All set for your lesson this afternoon?"

"Yeah, I've got all the stuff in the COOP room. Will you help me carry it onto the bus? Unless you're cutting class again today?"

"Oh, no—I mean, yeah, I'll be there, and I can definitely help you carry stuff."

"Thanks. What about *your* lesson? Do you at least have an idea?"

"I'm thinking of making it about Frida Kahlo. I can have the kids copy one of her self-portraits."

"Oh, that's cool. You're doing fourth grade, right? I think they'll like that."

Of course, it's not quite that simple. The art teacher has plenty of paper and pencils, but ideally the kids would get to color their drawings with oil pastels. I'll probably have to provide those, and I'm not sure how I'll afford them.

Makaila shoots me a quick glance out of the corner of her eye. "So, how is everything going with David?"

I sigh and tell her how I ran into him yesterday. "It was so awkward. I didn't know what to say to him. He said being around me is painful. I don't want to hurt him more than I already have."

"He's still gonna hurt. The boy is smitten."

Makaila pulls into a spot, and we walk into the overwhelming building. I'm glad to know I'm not the only one who feels like the immense population of this school is too much.

We part at the stairs, and I head to physics. David sees me as I walk in. Instead of looking away, he gives me a little wave. I give him a small smile. It's progress, I guess.

Between classes, I walk the crowded hallways by myself, missing the feel of David's hand in mine. I definitely can't cut COOP today, so I see David again there. He's sitting against the windows talking to Carlos. I find Makaila and slide in next to her.

She hands me a canvas bag. "This has the hot plate and pan. I've got the beakers and everything else in here." She nods at the tub beside her.

"You're going to do awesome. Steven loved your experiment."

"Yeah, but are twenty-one Stevens going to love it?"

"Yes, I know they will."

My prediction comes true. Makaila has all the kids up on their knees atop their stools trying to watch the water boil. When she walks around the lab with the pan of salt clumps and no water, their eyes are glued to her. After their teacher takes the third graders out of the lab, I go to the front to help Makaila clean up.

"That was amazing! I told you."

Makaila unplugs the hot plate, her face alight. "It was good, right?"

"Yes. A million times yes. They loved it. They loved you. You might even want to consider forgetting AP Chemistry and think about doing elementary."

She grimaces. "No. Just no. It was fine for one day, but I will take that high school job, thank you."

As I put the lids on the plastic containers of different mixtures, Ms. Mesa comes over to talk to Makaila. I put the rest of the materials into her tub and head toward the door where everyone else is gathered. David has been standing next to Carlos but sidles over to me.

"Hey. Makaila did awesome."

"Yeah. She's really good at this. She came over the other day to practice with Steven." I tell him how Steven reacted to her sink-or-float experiment, and David laughs. I miss that laugh so much. It brings a small gleam back into his eyes, and my stomach sinks. I need more of his laughter and light in my life.

"So, are you ready to go on Friday?"

I tell him that I think so, even though I actually do not have a solid plan yet.

"You'll do great."

He looks at me as if he wants to say more, but we just stand there in silence for almost an entire minute before Ms. Mesa ushers everyone out of the lab.

When I get home, I'm still thinking about the quiet way he looked at me. Steven and Dad are in the living room watching ESPN. I want to ask Dad how the therapy appointment went, but I'm not ready for any kind of disappointment. If he has a complaint about it or has decided it isn't for him, I don't want to hear it. Not now. I have too much on my mind to get wrapped up in his dysfunction at the moment. I grab an apple and go into the office.

I'm so far behind in everything right now. There's only one more week before Thanksgiving break, and the time off will give me a chance to catch up on the art show drawings. But first I have to get through my lesson at Las Positas this Friday.

I've decided to give a short lesson about Frida Kahlo and have the students copy one of her self-portraits. I go to Mom's file cabinet to see if I can find a simplified article about Frida as a quick reference. Just before Frida's folder, I find one labeled *France—Sarah.*

There are a few brochures and a long white envelope with *Sarah France $$* written on it. I open the envelope, and inside are printouts of bank statements with my name on them. On the inside of the envelope flap, Mom's written a username and password for the bank's website.

The most recent statement, from the month before Mom died, shows a balance of over eight hundred dollars.

She was saving money for the trip I wanted to take to France my senior year. Even though she would've preferred for me to focus on art in Latin American countries, and even though she would've loved nothing more than to take a family trip to Mexico or Guatemala, she set this money aside for France. For me.

I press the envelope to my chest and lower myself to the floor next to the file cabinet. I lean my head against the cool metal and close my eyes.

Even in death, my mom continues to show her love for me. I don't know if I will ever make it to France and even if I do one day, it will not be the same without her. But right now, this money can help me get through the two huge assignments that loom before me.

I have to buy oil pastels for Friday's lesson. I also need to get the drawings for the art show matted and figure out how to mount them. That all costs money, and this might be the only way to pay for it. Since the account's in my name and I have the online login information, I should be able to access it pretty easily.

"What are you doing on the floor?" Steven comes in and walks right over to me.

"Nothing." I push myself to my feet, put the envelope back in Mom's file cabinet and close the drawer. "I was just looking for something. What do you need?"

"Dad made grilled cheese. And I planned Thanksgiving."

I follow Steven out into the kitchen, where Dad is setting

the table. Steven takes a seat and holds up some index cards. "Dad will make the turkey and gravy." He pushes a card toward where Dad usually sits. "I'll do the pumpkin pie and canned corn. Sarah, you can make the mashed potatoes and stuffing." He hands me a card. "And no Stove Top. You have to make the good kind Mom always makes with the real bread."

I take the index card Steven offers me. He's scrawled *mashed potatoes and stuffing* with *no Stove Top* in parentheses. I guess we're having Thanksgiving. I wonder if Dad will really follow through on an actual turkey. He'll have to be a functioning human for multiple hours if he's going to accomplish it. I've never made a turkey, and I have zero intention of being in charge of one now. I admire Steven's determination to make this meal happen, but it wasn't something I was planning for or even hoping for.

Dad puts a plate with a grilled cheese sandwich in front of me. I am almost a hundred percent sure that this bread expired yesterday, but I don't say anything. I guess if there's no mold on it, it should be okay.

"Thanks, Dad." I turn the sandwich over and examine it. "How did your appointment go?" I've been wanting to ask him that since I came home, but I didn't know when the right time would be. This probably isn't the right time, but I just need to know.

He sits down across from me with his grilled cheese in front of him. "It was okay. The therapist is very encouraging. I go back next week. Once a week."

I think that's all I'll get out of him for now, so I let the conversation end there. After dinner, we all clean up. Steven takes the garbage out before heading upstairs to read the paper. I load the dishwasher while Dad wipes the table and countertops.

"Sarah, if you have some time, I can find that radio broadcast we were talking about the other day." Dad brings his laptop over to the table.

"Yeah, that sounds great." When he mentioned this the other night, I didn't think he would remember—I figured that it would be just another forgotten offer.

We sit down side by side while he pulls up the recording of the Radio Liberación, the fake broadcast that the CIA orchestrated to mislead the Guatemalan people about Jacobo Árbenz. Dad pauses the recording frequently to translate what's being said and to give me extra context. As I sit next to him, listening, I feel a little bit of my professor father making his way to the surface of whoever this man is now.

CHAPTER TWENTY-SIX

When Makaila picks me up, I give her a banana-berry smoothie in a disposable cup. "I hope you like smoothies. My dad made it this morning."

She takes a drink. "Yum. It's better than Smoothie King, and I do love my Smoothie King." She puts the cup in the cup holder and backs out of the driveway.

"I'll be sure to tell my dad that."

"How is he doing?"

"He's better. Thanks for asking." I don't want to go into all the details of it, but I do feel like I can honestly answer that he's better.

"You ready for tomorrow?"

"Actually, do you have a little time after school to take me to buy a few supplies?"

"I'm always up for a shopping trip."

"Thanks. I think I'll feel better about tomorrow once I've bought everything I need."

In physics, David waves at me and gives me a little smile. I keep sneaking glances at him throughout class and catch him looking my way once. These small moments soothe the brokenness I've been feeling.

During art class, Ms. Escamilla gives us time to work on our art projects. I start a new sketch based on one of Eugenio's photographs. It's of the group of people holding the "Viva Árbenz" sign. Right as class ends, Ms. Escamilla asks me to stay for a minute.

Unease pricks at the edges of my fingertips as I pack up. The bell rings, and the class clears out. I walk over to Ms. Escamilla's desk.

"Sarah, I talked to admin, and they are very firm on their political neutrality stance. They won't allow a petition to be presented at the art show. I explained your reasons to them, and I support your reasons. I'm sorry."

My disappointment quickly turns to anger, but I know Ms. Escamilla is just the messenger. Lashing out at her won't give me the result I want. So I keep my voice even. "What would happen if I do it anyway?"

She blinks at me and is quiet for a moment. "I don't know. I didn't ask that."

I think about my mother, about Frida. They did so much legwork in speaking out about this injustice. I have this moment to make a very small contribution to their efforts, and I can't waste it. "I feel very strongly about this. I think my art exhibit would be incomplete without this part. I don't feel that I can present the injustice of what happened to Guatemala without presenting at least one thing that can be done about it."

"Well, we can talk to Mr. Porter again. We can go together, after school."

"Okay, thank you."

Students for the next class start to shuffle in, so I leave, hoping I won't be late for COOP. I text Steven that I'll be home a little late.

Today is an easy day in COOP. We're filling out surveys to match us up with a class for next semester. Each of us will shadow a teacher at Las Positas twice a week, observing and helping in a classroom. Meanwhile, though, I still feel unprepared for tomorrow. Luckily, when I ask Ms. Mesa if I can borrow her iPad and adapter, she agrees. That just leaves the rest of the supplies for me to buy.

I ask Makaila if it's okay to stay after school a few minutes so I can talk to the vice-principal with Ms. Escamilla. She says she'll wait for me in the parking lot and we can go to the store after my meeting.

Four o'clock comes more quickly than I expected or wanted it to. Ms. Escamilla is already in the vice-principal's office when I walk in. She's seated in a chair opposite Mr. Porter, and I take the one next to her.

"This is Sarah Mosely. She's in my eleventh-grade advanced art class. She's a very talented artist and is preparing for the end-of-semester art showcase. As I told you earlier, she would like to present a petition at the art show."

Mr. Porter is a man I've never actually seen before. I imagine he's never seen me either. With three thousand students, it would be impossible for him to know every single one of us. He swivels in his chair. "Sarah, I explained to Ms. Escamilla that we have a policy of political neutrality at this school, and that is why we can't allow you to bring up a petition. The art show has to remain strictly about art."

I scoot up to the edge of my chair and press my fingers under my legs to keep them from shaking. "I understand about the policy, but I'm not endorsing a political candidate or a political party. My petition talks about renaming an airport that should've never been named after John Foster Dulles in the first place. John Foster Dulles, as the secretary of state, used lies and intimidation to overthrow a democratically elected president."

"I'm sorry, Sarah, but our policy stands."

"But this is about *ethics*. Dulles backed a dictator who killed people who disagreed with him. He supplied weapons used to commit genocide. At the time the airport was named after Dulles, not a lot of this was known. Now that the CIA documents are declassified and we know more, the ethical thing to do is to take his name off the airport."

"This is an *art* class." He turns to look at Ms. Escamilla. "Is this what you teach in *art* class?"

"I don't teach US history in art class, no. But students are encouraged to observe, to perceive, to express themselves creatively, and to communicate their ideas. And that is what Sarah is doing."

"Well, she can communicate her ideas through her art, not through a petition." He turns to me. "I'm sorry, Sarah. No petition."

He stands up, but I don't. I'm not done. I feel my mother's quiet urging. I know she's watching.

I free my hands from under my legs and place them on his desk. "Mr. Porter, I want to be a teacher one day, and in one of my early childhood classes, we talked about higher-order thinking. Students who are thinking at a low level can answer questions about facts, data. At the highest level, students create answers to problems, they present their own judgments. You should be glad that teachers at this school are getting their students to think at the highest level."

He looks at Ms. Escamilla like she's in charge of making me leave his office. She just shrugs.

"The answer is still no. If you bring up a petition, you'll be suspended for a week."

"But you don't even have a good reason!"

"A week's suspension *and* a failing grade on the assignment." He walks over to the door and opens it.

Ms. Escamilla stands up now. "No. Her grade can't be affected by behavior. Those are separate issues. Her grade will be based on her work, not on anything else."

"Fine. A week's suspension. That's all the time I've got, ladies."

I finally stand up and follow Ms. Escamilla out of the office. Mr. Porter closes the door behind us.

"I'm sorry, Sarah. There's no changing his mind."

"That's okay. I said what I had to say."

We walk out of the admin area and into the hallway. "What are you going to do?" Ms. Escamilla asks me.

"I have to do the petition."

"You're willing to get suspended?"

"It's not about me. It's for my mom." I wasn't expecting my voice to catch. I clear my throat. "She died last year. She taught Latin American history, and she tried to teach me about it. And I didn't want to listen. I wasn't interested. It was her life's work. So I have to do this now. Because she can't."

Ms. Escamilla looks at me and presses her lips together. "Okay. Well, I support you, Sarah."

"Thank you. Can I present last at the show? I don't want to disrupt anyone else's presentation."

"Yes, I'll put you last on the program." She rubs the side of my arm. "Your mama would be so proud of you."

CHAPTER TWENTY-SEVEN

Makaila is waiting for me by her car, scrolling through her phone. As I approach, she tries to read my face, but I don't know what's there. Disappointment that I couldn't convince Mr. Porter? Satisfaction that I didn't back down from the fight? Anxiety about going against a policy and facing suspension?

"Well?" Makaila holds up both hands, her phone in one of them.

"He still said no, but I'm going to do the petition anyway. Which means I'll be suspended for a week."

"Sarah! A week!" She shakes her head. "What will your dad say?"

"I can't think about that. He said he'll support me no matter what. But even if he doesn't, I just feel like I have to do it. For my mom. This was something she cared about, and I'm going to do what I can."

"Come here." Makaila moves in and puts her arms around me. "You've got this."

I wrap my arms around her and release the tears I've been fighting back since Mr. Porter invited me into his office. We pull apart, and I wipe my face. "Thank you. You've been such a good friend."

"When the fight picks you, you need a good friend. When I'm called to fight my fights, I know you'll have my back."

I nod, still wiping away my tears. "Always."

"Now let's go get these art supplies. You've got another fight coming up tomorrow, trying to get these third graders to do what you say!"

I have new texts from Steven.

STEVEN: The groceries came

STEVEN: Dad and I are putting them away now

STEVEN: Dad's making lasagna for dinner

His last message is a picture of Garfield diving into a pan of lasagna. I laugh and show it to Makaila, who rolls her eyes. I don't know if she's over Steven thwarting her sink-or-float experiment with his overconfidence. She takes me to buy several sets of oil pastels, and I buy us milkshakes at Whataburger to thank her. *Milkshakes on Mom*, I think when I pay at the counter. This sweet treat is possible because of the money Mom set aside for me, and it's nice to be able to do a little something for Makaila. It's also nice to be able to do something for me.

The nerves begin as soon as I wake up. A tingling sensation starts at the edges of my fingers and toes and spreads throughout my body. Today I'll be teaching an entire class. It's not the kids that make me nervous. They're basically just a bunch of Stevens; I'm used to that. But my COOP classmates, the art teacher, and Ms. Mesa will be standing in the back, watching my every move.

The school day starts with encouraging words from Makaila when she picks me up. A smile from David in physics also bolsters my spirits. When we're on the bus on the way to Las Positas Elementary, the nerves kick in again.

The art room at Las Positas Elementary has six large tables with tall stools surrounding them. There's a large space at the front of the room with a smartboard and a long table. The art teacher, Ms. Blake, introduces me and moves aside. Students watch me from their tall stools while my classmates and Ms. Mesa fill the space in the back of the room.

I plug Ms. Mesa's iPad into Ms. Blake's smartboard. "Would you all like to see a picture of a painting that just recently sold for over thirty million dollars?"

"Whoa!"

"What?"

"Million?"

I show them an image of one of Frida Kahlo's paintings. "Someone bought this for thirty-nine million dollars. Does anyone recognize this artist?"

One student raises her hand. "My mom has a T-shirt with that lady on it."

"She looks like the lady in the movie *Coco*," says another student.

I go to the next image, an early photograph of Frida. "This is Frida Kahlo. She was a Mexican artist. She loved to do self-portraits because she said that she was the subject she knew best. She didn't paint herself exactly the way she looked in real life, though. She painted herself the way she saw herself and wanted to be seen." I tell them a little bit about Frida's life, and they ask a few questions. I pass out art paper to each student and explain the project. "We're going to make a portrait of Frida Kahlo."

One girl in the front raises her hand. "Can I sell mine for

thirty million dollars?" Her classmates laugh and she adds, "Just saying."

"You can do whatever you like with your portrait. It'll be your version of Frida—how *you* see her, what *you* want to show and emphasize. That means it's your own creation. It's as much about you as it is about her."

I show them how to get started. "Fold the paper twice, once hamburger style and once hotdog style." I fold my paper in half lengthwise and then in half the other way. I walk around to make sure everyone is on track. I stop to help a little boy who can't fold straight. I try not to look over at my COOP classmates.

Next, I use the iPad to show the kids each step to make their drawing, pausing frequently so they can follow along. After we've all finished with Frida's facial features, I pass out a set of oil pastels to each table so the kids can color their portraits. As I walk around, I see that the students have all drawn Frida differently. Some have made a wide face, others a narrow face. A few students have thinned out her eyebrows while one has made them so wide that they cover half her face.

Students get right to work coloring, passing colors back and forth and showing off their work. I help those who've been left behind.

Most have finished by the time we have to clean up. I collect the sets of oil pastels as Ms. Blake's students line up to go back to their classroom.

"These look amazing," Ms. Blake tells me. "We're going to hang these up in the hall. I can tell the kids had a lot of fun. Thank you, Sarah."

"Thank you! You have a wonderful class."

I'm beaming by the time Makaila meets me halfway to the door. "You killed it! They were so into that."

"I think the thirty million got their attention."

"It got my attention too. Is that for real? That picture sold for thirty-nine million?"

"Yeah. It's not even one of her best, I don't think."

"I think I'm in the wrong field. I wonder if it's too late to change to art."

I laugh. "There aren't too many artists who make that kind of money. You've heard the term 'starving artist,' right? I think you're better off sticking to chemistry."

David stands at the door. The vivid smile I chased away is back, and his eyes have a trace of the sparkle I haven't seen for a while. "Sarah, that was really good. The kids loved it." He turns to walk with Makaila and me toward the school's main entrance, since it's time to head back to Richards.

"Thank you. I was really nervous."

David shakes his head. "You're a natural with kids. I knew that the first time I saw you with Steven."

"Thanks." I think back to that day at the football game when he came to sit with us. I called him an interloper, but I've loved his gentle presence in my life ever since. There's so much I want to say to him, but none of the words seem adequate. *I'm sorry. I miss you. I love you. I want you.* All my words get caught in my heart, and I can't say anything.

David holds the door open for Makaila and me, and we thank him.

Makaila senses the awkward moment and steps in. "I was telling Sarah that I might pick up a paintbrush if there's thirty-nine million dollars in that line of work."

"Ahh, but you may never see that amount in your lifetime. Your paintings might only get super valuable when you die."

Once we're on the bus, he goes off to sit with Carlos while

Makaila and I snag seats in the front. "You okay?" she asks me.

"I don't know. It just doesn't feel right. David's being nice to me now, but in the same way he's nice to everyone, and I don't know if I like that any better. Maybe he doesn't even care anymore."

"Girl, of course he cares. He just doesn't know what to do with it right now."

I turn around to look at David. He's talking to Carlos. *I don't know what to do with it right now either.*

CHAPTER TWENTY-EIGHT

O ver the next two weeks, I spend all my spare time working on my art project. Knowing that I still have most of the money Mom saved for me has given me the guts to close my Etsy shop, at least for the time being, so that I don't have to juggle extra work. I finish my sketches of the Árbenz supporters and the troops on the trucks. I do more research online and draft my presentation for the showcase. And I finally decide on my last sketch.

The week of Thanksgiving, Vic volunteers to help my dad make my display for the pieces. The two of them go to the hardware store and buy some PVC pipe. Dad designs a pole that will be inserted into a base on the ground. It will hold two sketches and can be easily lifted out. Together, Dad and Vic make four of these. Dad has also asked Vic to bring the display to school in his pickup on the day of the showcase.

Everyone gathering to support me in this moment fills me with a sense of relief. Right now, for the first time since Mom died, the only person I have to worry about is myself, and that feels so freeing. Maybe one day soon, it'll start to feel natural again.

Meanwhile, Dad's going to therapy every week, and Vic is going to put Dad in touch with a friend of his who's an AA sponsor. I'm not sure I see my dad going to AA meetings on the regular, but his willingness to talk to this sponsor is another tiny step that feels hopeful.

Waking up on Thanksgiving has always meant the scent of cinnamon wafting through the house. Mom used to make homemade cinnamon rolls every Thanksgiving morning. She would move the TV to the kitchen and watch the Macy's Thanksgiving Day parade as she baked. This morning, there will be no cinnamon rolls and no parade.

I lie in bed and text Alexa a long feel-sorry-for-me text that I wouldn't usually write. She sends me two little bears hugging and says she can't wait to see me tomorrow. We keep texting until I hear Steven softly knocking on my door.

"Sarah, are you awake?" he whispers.

"Yes."

He opens the door and tosses himself at the foot of my bed. "I can't open this."

I sit up and lean against the headboard. He holds out a refrigerated can of cinnamon rolls.

"I don't know how to make Mom's cinnamon rolls, but I saw these on a commercial. I had Dad add them to the grocery order this week."

I take the can from him. He's torn off most of the paper. "You have to press on this line with a spoon or something."

He gets me a spoon, and I press it against the can. It opens with a pop and some of the dough squeezes out the side.

"Wow. That's cool." Steven grabs it from me and heads to the door.

"I'll help you make those." I crawl out of bed and walk down the stairs behind him. "We have to preheat the oven first."

In the kitchen, I turn on the oven and Steven finishes opening the can and puts the circles of dough in a baking pan.

When I open the refrigerator, I see the packaged turkey still sitting on the bottom shelf. Dad hasn't even opened it, much less seasoned or prepared it. Should we just give up on this charade, pretend it isn't Thanksgiving?

We won't even be able to enjoy it without Mom. We'll be seeing her empty spot at the table, missing her insistence that each of us say what we're grateful for.

"Is Dad awake?" I ask.

"No. I'm going to wake him up in an hour to start the turkey. Maybe the smell of these cinnamon rolls will wake him. That used to wake me up."

I don't know how it is that this whole holiday came to rest on the tiny shoulders of an eight-year-old.

As I watch my little brother, in his too-short pajamas, trying to space the cinnamon rolls apart equally in the little pan, I know that he is doing his best to keep Mom's traditions alive.

I go into the living room, unplug the TV and bring it into the kitchen, where I place it on top of the counter.

"You're putting the parade on?" Steven turns to look at me.

"Yeah, we have to watch the parade."

His eyes light up. "Like when Mom was here."

We sit at the table and watch the parade as we wait for the oven timer. This is such a familiar experience, even without the sound of a rolling pin moving against my mother's perfect dough. I put my arm around Steven and pull him toward me. Her loss is so pronounced right now; every missing sound emphasizes this terrible thing that has happened to our family.

The timer goes off, and I bring the pan of hot cinnamon rolls to the table. Steven opens the plastic pouch of icing with his teeth and spreads it onto the rolls. This will not compare to Mom's homemade icing.

It wasn't just the rolls or the icing. It isn't any one thing that makes my heart ache, but the totality of who she was. She loved us so much, and she would make each day better by just being present.

I lick the icing off a roll. "This is good, Steven."

Steven takes in a mouthful. "Would Mom be proud?"

"Yes, very proud."

The parade is almost over, and we haven't seen or heard Dad.

"Here comes Mom's favorite part. Santa's coming." Steven pushes himself up to his knees and gets closer to the TV.

If Thanksgiving without Mom is this painful, I cannot imagine what Christmas will feel like.

The parade ends as Steven and I eat the rest of the cinnamon rolls. Dad finally comes downstairs in his pajamas and slippered feet. Steven and I both watch him to see what he's going to do. Is he going to start on the turkey—do his best, like we're doing, to get through this gloomy day? Or will he dissolve into the weepy and dejected Dad we've come to expect?

He takes the wrapped-up turkey out of the refrigerator and sets it in the sink. The oven is still warm from Steven's rolls, so when Dad preheats it, it doesn't take long to beep again. Dad takes out a roasting pan and puts it next to the sink. He uses a long knife to cut open the plastic and places the turkey straight onto the pan. Without even a pinch of salt, he shoves the pan into the oven and sets a timer.

"Should be about two and a half hours." He turns around

and heads back upstairs without so much as throwing away the gross, bloody plastic packaging the bird came in.

I shake my head. I am not cleaning up that mess. "Come on, Steven. Let's put the TV back in the living room and we can watch the dog show."

"But what about the other Thanksgiving food?"

"We still have time to make it. The potatoes don't take long, and we can put the stuffing in after the turkey's done cooking."

Steven doesn't need more convincing. He grabs two flannel blankets out of the hall closet and brings them over to the couch. We get comfortable under the blankets and watch the National Dog Show.

Afterward, I make Steven change out of his pajamas while I take a shower. Dad hasn't emerged from his room yet, and there's about half an hour before the oven timer will go off. I follow Mom's recipes for the mashed potatoes and stuffing. Steven opens the cans of corn and unwraps the store-bought pumpkin pie. He sets the table with the wrinkled linen napkins Mom would always use on special occasions.

The timer for the turkey goes off, and Dad reappears. He's now wearing a charcoal-gray V-neck sweater over a white T-shirt. His hair is sopping wet and combed back, and his eyes are swollen and red. He puts on oven mitts and takes the turkey out. I put the stuffing into the oven and adjust the temperature.

"I'm going to let this sit for a little bit before I start carving it." Dad leaves the roasting pan on top of the stove and turns to look at me. "This is going to be really hard." His voice wavers and his eyes drop.

"I know. For Steven and me too." It sucks that I have to say that to him. He isn't the only one suffering, feeling such a great loss, such an emptiness on this day when we're somehow supposed to celebrate gratitude. Steven, very quiet for once, watches us as he stirs the corn.

Dad looks back up at me. "Yeah. We just have to make the best of it. It's what she would have wanted." He closes the gap between us, and I let him hug me. For the first time since she died, *he* is the one comforting *me*. I am eight years old again and have just lost the school art competition, and he is helping me feel like everything is going to be okay. A rush of tears escapes me.

Steven puts his spoon down and comes over to where we're standing. He throws his arms around both of us and squeezes.

It is Thanksgiving, and I don't feel particularly thankful for much. I feel more hopeful than thankful. There is hope that my dad will be my dad again. Even though our kitchen is not filled with the sounds and scents of every Thanksgiving before today, and even though we only have a store-bought pie, my thrown-together stuffing, and an unseasoned turkey to put on our table, I have hope that my dad will keep going to therapy each week, that he will venture out of his room and away from his alcohol, that the three of us will figure out how to be a family.

I throw my hoodie on and go outside to wait for Alexa. I haven't seen her since she was home for the summer, and I've missed her so much. She pulls her red Honda into my driveway and runs over to me. She's wearing a short jacket with a furry hood and has her long black hair in a high ponytail.

She pulls me into a tight hug. "It's so good to see you. Your hair is getting so long—I love your curls." She pulls gently on a strand of my hair. "I brought Starbucks!" She ducks back into her car, slings a bag over her shoulder, and retrieves two coffees from the drink holders, handing one to me. "Upside-down caramel macchiato."

"My favorite! I haven't had one of these in forever." I take a sip right away. Alexa and I used to get one of these at least once a week at PFA. "Mmmm. I've missed these. And I missed you more."

We go to my room and close the door behind us. Alexa kicks her shoes off and sits cross-legged on my bed to drink her cold foam iced cappuccino. "So what is up with David these days?"

"I don't know. He's back to making eye contact, so that's good."

"Are you going to get back together with him?"

"I mean . . . I want to, but I don't know if I can promise that things will be any different—that I'll be any less stressed or distracted or sad. I don't even know for sure that my dad is getting better."

"Just tell David what you told me, and let him decide whether he wants to be with you the way you are right now. Call him today."

I lean back in bed and take another joyous sip of perfection in a cup. "I can't. He has a basketball game today. Their season started last week."

"A basketball game? Home or away?"

I shrug, pretending not to know. I know. Of course I know. "I think it's a home game."

She gets off the bed and sprints to the door. "Steven!"

Steven comes down the hallway. "Alexa?"

"Get your shoes. We're going to David's basketball game."

"Okay! I'm going to wear the Richards sweatshirt David bought me."

I stay on my bed. "I'm not going," I say to Alexa. "That would be weird."

"Come on. We're going." Alexa points at me with the hand she's still holding her cup with. "And put on *your* Richards sweatshirt."

"I don't even have one." I roll my eyes and slump deeper into my bed.

She puts her cup down on my desk and pulls out some of my drawing paper. "David Garza, right?"

"What are you doing?" I hop off my bed.

She has one of my thick Sharpies and is writing David's name on one of my large sheets of drawing paper. "What's his number?"

"His number? I don't—"

"Twenty-seven." Steven walks in wearing his Richards High School sweatshirt. He has combed his hair, has put his shoes on, and is firmly on Alexa's side. "I can't believe you didn't tell me about David's game, Sarah. That's not cool."

"Not cool, Sarah," Alexa says. "Let's go. I'm driving."

I text Dad that Steven and I are going to the basketball game with Alexa, and I do as I'm told.

We get to the school just before the start of the game, when the players are warming up. One side of the gym is covered in green and white for the Richards Bears. Steven shouts at David, trying to get his attention above the loud music, and I just want to crawl under a rock.

David is taking a layup. He's wearing green basketball shorts lined with white stripes and a green Richards jersey. I've never seen him wear his uniform before, and I can't look away from him, from his fluid movements as he dribbles the ball. He gets his own rebound and dribbles to center court.

We sit in the front row, and Steven continues shouting David's name. Eventually David hears him and looks over at us, a stunned expression on his face. But he recovers enough to smile at Steven and give him a little salute. Alexa hands Steven her homemade sign, and Steven holds it up above his head. David laughs, gives Steven a thumbs up, and dribbles the ball back toward the basket.

Alexa puts her arm around me. "Your man is a hottie, Sarah."

I roll my eyes. "He's more than a hottie. He's really sweet."

"Okay, so please fix this. I want to see you happy."

"I'll try. Do you think I've got a chance?"

"Are you kidding? His eyes lit up when he saw you." She stands up and starts yelling, "Go Bears!"

The players are announced and take their places.

"David is a starter. That means he's really good." Steven holds up the sign again.

The game clock starts, and Steven is right. David is really good. There's a lot of scoring and David is in double digits right away. Alexa squeezes my arm every time he scores like I had anything to do with it. Steven goes hoarse yelling David's name whenever he so much as touches the ball. At halftime, Alexa and Steven go get snacks, and we munch on popcorn and nachos during the second half. When the game is over, the Richards Bears have won. They walk past the opposing team, giving them high fives, and I catch David looking my way.

"David!" Steven jumps to his feet and waves.

David jogs over to us. "Hey, Steven. Thanks for coming to my game."

"We made a sign with your number." He holds up the now-bent sign.

"Thanks. I appreciated all your cheering." He turns to Alexa. "Hi, you're Alexa, right? We met on FaceTime, remember?"

"I remember! Good game."

"Thanks. And thank you for coming."

Steven reinserts himself into the conversation. "It was all Alexa's idea. She had to talk Sarah into coming."

Alexa grabs Steven by the neck of his sweatshirt. "Come on, Steven. Let's throw away our garbage."

Neither of us looks in their direction as they walk away. "It was a really good game," I tell David. "You're very good."

"Thank you. I'm glad you came even if Alexa had to talk you into it."

I pull at my fingers. "I just didn't know if you'd want to see me."

"I always want to see you."

I take a deep breath. "I'm really sorry. I feel like I messed everything up."

"Hey, Garza," comes a voice across the gym. "Coach wants to talk to everyone."

David turns around to respond to his teammate. "Okay, be right there." To me, he says, "I have to go, but can we find a time to talk?"

"Yeah, for sure."

"Thanks. Bye, Sarah." David turns around and jogs toward where the rest of his team is standing.

Alexa and Steven reappear as if on cue. "So, how did it go?" Alexa asks.

"Okay. He was glad we came. He wants to talk soon."

"Awesome. Mission accomplished."

"What mission?" Steven asks.

"The mission of getting them back together!"

Steven shuffles behind us. "Why? What happened?"

"Never mind," I say. Alexa and I steer him out of the gym.

Steven heaves a sigh. "I never know anything that is going on."

When we get home, Steven turns on ESPN while Alexa and I head back upstairs.

"So, tell me about your art show," Alexa says, leaning back on my pillows. "That's coming up, right?"

"Yeah, it's next week. On Friday."

"Okay, I'm coming back down. I don't want to miss it."

"That would be awesome. I'm going to need all the friends I can get that night." I tell her about my meeting with Mr. Porter, about the threat of a one-week suspension.

Her eyes go wide and she sits up. "And you're going to do it anyway?"

"I have to."

I show her the drawings, explaining my great-grandfather's story and the story of Guatemala. We spend the rest of the day talking about these events, about injustices in our history, and about our very small part in doing something about it.

CHAPTER TWENTY-NINE

I haven't seen David since the game on Friday. In physics on Monday morning, we quietly agree to cut COOP so we can talk in private. COOP has become a free period now that each of us has taught our class. We're supposed to be doing a research paper. Ms. Mesa will give us the whole class period to work on this every day for the rest of the semester, knowing our lives will get busier in January when we start going to our assigned elementary classrooms twice a week.

At the start of fourth period, we meet in the courtyard near the picnic tables. David sits down on one of the benches. "Are you cold? It's getting a little cold."

"It's not real cold, just Texas cold, as Steven would say." I sit down next to him, leaving a few inches between us.

"How is Steven? And how's your dad?"

"Steven is doing okay. He bounced back pretty well after . . . that night. He's doing a good job holding us all together. He singlehandedly planned Thanksgiving and gave us all food assignments."

"Sounds like Steven."

"My dad's doing a little better too, I think."

"I'm glad. You've been dealing with a lot, and I hope it's better for you."

I turn to look him straight in the eye. "I am so sorry for how I treated you."

"I know. It really hurt, but I get that your priority is your family. I can't even begin to understand what you're going through."

"But you just wanted to be there for me. And I wish I could've let myself believe you when you told me that. I miss you."

David's lips ease into a tentative half smile.

"A lot. I miss you a lot."

"I miss you too, Sarah."

I dig through my backpack and pull out the sketch of David I started the day he led the PE class at Las Positas Elementary. "This is for you."

His half-smile expands into one of his full-length ones, the kind that causes the corners of his eyes to crease, as he stares at the sketch. His eyes dart down to what I wrote at the bottom: *I'm sorry. I miss you. I love you. I want you.*

"I really love you, Sarah. I want to try again."

"I want to try again too."

Holding the sketch between us, he leans in to press his forehead against mine. "I love this picture. Thank you."

"You looked so good that day. I loved the shorts you were wearing. I had to immortalize them."

He laughs. "I will wear those shorts for you any day." He kisses me, bringing his hands up to frame my face. I scoot as close to him as I can on the bench and wrap my arms around his waist. The coolness of the air subsides.

The bell rings.

"Should we skip lunch and just stay here kissing?" I ask.

"I wish. I have a test next period, so I need to eat and finish studying. Can I see you after school, though?"

I unwrap my arms from him and stand up. "Yeah. Makaila has been taking me home after school. I'm supposed to get my car back tomorrow."

"Can I take you home today then?"

"Okay, I'll text Makaila."

He takes my hand, and we walk back inside together. He holds my sketch in his other hand.

CHAPTER THIRTY

I would rather face those fourth graders in art class a hundred times over than have to present at the art show today. But Alexa texted me that she's on her way, and Vic has just arrived to help me load my mobile display into the back of his pickup. "Laura wanted to come, but she had to take the twins to a birthday party. She sent you these." He hands me a bouquet of mixed flowers.

"Thank you. That was so nice of her." I haven't seen Laura for a while. I suspect that Dad's incessant neediness burned her out over the last few months. Sometimes I wonder if she ever gets frustrated that we rely on Vic so much. "Let me go put them in water."

Under our sink, there's an assortment of vases that I tucked there to get them out of sight after Mom died. So many flowers were sent, and as they withered, dried, and slumped, I would throw the flowers away and put another vase under the sink.

I push them aside to reach the one in the back that's different, more familiar. This was Mom's go-to vase whenever she bought flowers. It's not fancy or expensive. It's a slender, clear glass cylinder with no embellishments, but with so many memories attached. As I fill it with water and place the bouquet inside, the sudden memories of my mom give me the push I need to get through today.

Dad, Vic, and Steven are already in the truck waiting for me, and I hop in the back with Steven. I'm grateful for his jabbering as we head to school.

"So, if Sarah gets suspended, will it go on her permanent record?"

"No, Steven," I say.

"So, she just gets to stay home from school for a whole week and do what? Sleep in and watch TV? That's not fair."

"Steven, she's not doing it for fun, she's making a point." Dad looks at me through the mirror on the visor in front of him. "And your mom would be proud of her."

I smile at him.

Vic pulls into a parking spot, and he and Dad unload the mobile display while Steven helps me carry the matted sketches.

"Sarah!" Alexa's voice makes me jump. She runs across the parking lot, her parents trailing her at a normal pace. Alexa wraps her arms around me and kisses my cheek. "Let me help you." She takes two of the sketches.

The air in the cafeteria feels cold, like someone cranked up the air conditioning on this already frigid December day. There are so many people here already—staff, students, their families, and I guess some random community members too. I spot Señora Dominguez, who waves to me.

I find my assigned spot and help Vic and my dad assemble the display. We place the matted sketches in order.

Alexa's parents find some people they know and stay in the background. I'm grateful to count them as two more people who've come here just for me, to support me on this stressful day.

David comes over, wheeling a portable speaker. He puts his hand on my hip as he kisses my cheek. His lips warm my skin and his touch helps calm my nerves. "Hey. You feeling good?"

"Super nervous."

"You're going to do awesome. You have so many people here who love you." He nods at Dad and Vic, who both nod back.

David clips a microphone to my shirt, and we test it with the speaker. "Steven, you'll be in charge of this," David tells my brother, gesturing to the speaker. Steven nods solemnly.

Makaila comes over. "These came out so good. You're going to do fantastic."

"Thank you." I introduce Makaila to Alexa, and they join David off to the side of my display, ready to execute what Makaila calls "the getaway plan" if I get run out of here.

There must be hundreds of people here now. As Ms. Escamilla welcomes the public and introduces the show, I spot Mr. Porter standing off to one side. He eyes me, but I look away from him.

My classmate Colton goes first. He's painted iconic scenes from the Civil Rights Movement and talks about the historical context of each image. Stephanie, a girl I've never talked to, follows Colton. She's painted stretches of highways in Texas with wildflowers and bluebonnets. Stephanie explains that former first lady Lady Bird Johnson promoted the planting of wildflowers along highways. I've seen these wildflowers along I-35 all my life, every springtime. Memories of my mom trying to take pictures of the red, yellow, and blue flowers as we drove past come flooding back as Stephanie talks.

There are also some mixed-media displays, and my classmate Maritza has created a series of small metal sculptures. Each student takes their turn talking about their artwork, while the massive audience shuffles and shifts toward each new display.

And now, it's my turn.

Ms. Escamilla hands me the microphone everyone's been using, but I decline it. I tell her I have my own microphone, and I turn it on.

Mr. Porter has edged closer to me, his arms crossed.

"My display is called 'Rotten Fruit.' It's a story told through photographs taken by my great-grandfather, Eugenio Alvarado. He's shown in this first sketch. He left behind photographs that he took of historical events that he experienced in Guatemala." I point to the next sketch. "This is the United Fruit Company. It was an American banana company that bought up massive amounts of land in Guatemala in the 1930s. The Guatemalan government sold land to this company at very low prices, and the heads of the company undervalued their land so they could pay lower taxes."

Mr. Porter's hands go into the pockets of his pleated khakis and he meets my eyes with raised eyebrows. I pause for a moment as he stares me down.

I search for David. His smiling eyes, full of encouragement, propel me to continue.

"Along with not paying their fair share of taxes, this company also didn't pay fair wages and treated its employees poorly." I point to two sketches of the workers on the plantation. "This next image shows supporters of Jacobo Árbenz, Guatemala's democratically elected president, who took office in 1950. He really looked up to Franklin Delano Roosevelt, the US president in the 1940s. FDR's policies had created a lot of jobs and had done a lot to help people who were struggling. Árbenz wanted to bring about similar reforms in Guatemala that would help people and make the economy stronger—reforms like supporting labor unions, fair wages, and better working conditions. After he was elected, he had the

Guatemalan government buy unused land to give it to local farmers, especially Indigenous people. But there were powerful people who opposed all this."

I look out at the audience—at my dad, whose attention is completely on me. He gives me a smile, an encouragement I'm no longer used to. This is what fathers are supposed to do, what my father has not done in a long time. It comes at the exact moment I need it, as Mr. Porter clears his throat.

I forge ahead. "The United Fruit Company had supporters in high places, high up in the Eisenhower administration, including John Foster Dulles, the secretary of state, and his brother, Allen Dulles, the head of the CIA. They were angry about United Fruit losing land to this program. The company was compensated for the land the government redistributed, but remember, they had purposely undervalued their land to get out of paying taxes, so when the government bought it from them, they didn't get as much money as they wanted."

I move over to point at the sketch of the men holding rifles. "The supporters of United Fruit convinced the Eisenhower administration to overthrow President Árbenz. The US government spread misinformation that Árbenz was a communist." I recount how the CIA used psychological warfare to turn people against Árbenz. I show the sketch of the planes used to scare the Guatemalan people.

As I finish telling the story of the coup, I move to the last sketch, which is a mass grave that holds the remains of many victims of genocide. I've drawn a massive pile of bones. Skulls of different sizes. Some white, some gray. This is not based on one of my great-grandfather's photographs. It's inspired by an image I found on the Internet, but I decided to use it as the concluding piece of my presentation. When I first saw that image,

I couldn't shake the thought of how these bodies were carelessly and cruelly thrown on top of each other.

I describe the thirty-six-year civil war, explaining how the CIA coached the Guatemalan military on brutal counterinsurgency tactics that included the slaughter of civilians. I explain how the US government gave millions of dollars in aid to Guatemala even though it knew about the Guatemalan government's human rights violations.

"This is US history that we don't learn about in school. Students should know that the United States overthrew a democratically elected president and gave millions of dollars to fund the genocide of over two hundred thousand people in Guatemala."

I look out at the audience, wondering if I'm boring them or offending them. After all, they came here to look at art.

"Look, I know that the US has done some horrible things throughout history. This is nothing new. But now that we know better, we should do better. Even though none of that history can be undone, there are things we can do differently going forward. For example, the Dulles International Airport in Washington, DC, is named after John Foster Dulles, who orchestrated this overthrow of a democracy. Over twenty million people fly through this airport every year. It should not be named after this man."

Mr. Porter signals to Ms. Escamilla, who shrugs at him.

I turn back to the crowd. "There is a petition to rename—"

Mr. Porter comes to stand in front of me. "I'm sorry, but we are going to have to end the art show now. Thank you, everyone, for coming out today."

I step around Mr. Porter and turn up the volume on my microphone. I hold up a clipboard with the petition. "Please sign this petition to rename the Dulles International Airport."

Mr. Porter turns around to face me. "Sarah, you are suspended. For a week. You need to stop now."

I take two steps away from him. "If you are interested in signing this petition please meet me outside."

Mr. Porter turns back to the crowd. "Ladies and gentlemen, I apologize for Sarah's misguided behavior. She was warned not to do this."

Steven moves with me toward the door, pulling the speaker behind him. Makaila, David, and Alexa go to the display and pick up the poles holding my matted sketches. David takes two—one pole in each hand. Together, the three of them carry my artwork away from the other displays and follow me.

"It is okay to say that something is wrong," I say as I walk. "When the airport was named, not all of this information was well known. In 1997, documents about US involvement in Guatemala were declassified, and now we know. Now we know. So let's do something. Please come outside to sign the petition."

Outside the school, David, Makaila, and Alexa set up my sketches at the edge of the parking lot. Dad and Vic and Alexa's parents surround me.

Alexa's mother takes the clipboard from my hands. "Wonderful work, Sarah." She signs the petition and hands it to her husband, who signs it and returns it to me.

I look toward the door to see if anyone else is coming, but only those who know me directly have ventured outside. Alexa signs the petition and holds the clipboard while David and Makaila sign too. I'm grateful for their support, but I wonder if my words reached anyone else. There were hundreds of people inside.

The door swings open, and Colton comes out with some of the other art class students behind him. Alexa walks over to them with the petition, and they all sign it. At least I have several more signatures, but were they worth getting suspended for?

I feel the need to say something more. After all, David went through all the trouble of bringing his portable microphone and speaker. "Thank you to those who've signed the petition. It really means a lot. I found this petition in some of my mother's files. She passed away a few months ago, and I would like to honor her memory by continuing something that was very meaningful to her."

The door opens again, and a crowd floods outside. Not everyone leaving the art show is walking toward me—some are just heading to their cars in the parking lot behind me. But dozens, maybe close to a hundred, line up behind the person currently signing the petition. Makaila approaches the crowd and hands out cards with a QR code that will take them to the online petition. I told Makaila we wouldn't need many, but she insisted on printing out two dozen.

People take the cards and scan the code to sign the petition, passing the cards on to others when they're finished. Makaila looks over at me and gives me a thumbs-up.

Colton comes over to me. "Great job, Sarah. I love how you used the petition to drive your point home. I can think of a few places I would like to see renamed. Can I get with you next week and throw some ideas around?"

"Yeah, for sure! Thank you for signing the airport petition."

"You got it." He turns around and heads back inside.

Students, parents, grandparents walk by me with supportive words. Makaila and Alexa are working the crowd, helping people sign, while David guards my sketches.

I look over at him, and I could swear that his smile shines brighter than the stars beginning to emerge in the sky. I just love him so much.

Alexa holds up her phone to me. "Instagram post is getting a lot of traction from PFA. Ten students from PFA have commented that they signed it online already! Fifteen people have already retweeted it on Twitter."

I bring my hands to my heart in thanks, and she turns right back to her phone for more social media management.

Dad comes over once the crowd begins to thin out. There are tears in his eyes, but not the same kind of tears I've seen there so often over the past few months. "Your mom is so proud of you, Sarah. I don't think she could have imagined all you've done. You searched her heart, everything she ever felt about Guatemala and her grandfather's experiences. You told his story, the story of his country and her heritage."

I put one arm around him and the other around Steven. Even though Mom is not here, I still feel her. She lives on in me, in this story I told tonight, and in the work I'm not done with.

AUTHOR'S NOTE

In 1959, just four days after John Foster Dulles passed away, Republican senator Homer E. Capehart introduced a bill to name a planned new airport in Washington, DC, after Dulles. While the airport was under construction, there were conversations about naming it Washington International Airport instead so that international travelers could more easily recognize it (since *Dulles* could easily be mistaken for *Dallas*). After pushback from the Dulles family, it was named Dulles International Airport when it opened in 1962. Later it was renamed Washington Dulles International Airport for clarity. In 1990, Republican senator Robert Dole introduced a resolution to rename the airport after President Eisenhower. The Dulles family protested, and the name was not changed.

The current movement to rename Dulles International Airport was not Sarah's idea, nor was it her mother's. There are several online petitions to rename this airport, which anyone who is interested can sign. There are also other ways to speak out about this issue. Those who would like to see this airport renamed after a more deserving individual can contact their US senators and representatives.

QUESTIONS FOR DISCUSSION

1. How does Sarah's mother's death impact Sarah's daily life six months later?

2. From Sarah's point of view, her dad's love for her and Steven seems to have died with Sarah's mom. What has given Sarah this impression? Why do you think Sarah's dad is behaving this way?

3. Why is Sarah initially wary of David? What does this show about her priorities and about her emotional state right now?

4. What ended Sarah's friendship with Brad in sixth grade? Contrast Brad's behavior with the ways David shows Sarah that he likes and cares about her.

5. How does David treat Steven, and what does this reveal about his character?

6. When Sarah decides to make her art project about the CIA coup in Guatemala, she reflects, "How has any of this impacted me personally? It hasn't, I don't think." In what ways *has* this history shaped her life without her being aware of it?

7. How do Frida Kahlo's and Diego Rivera's activism influence Sarah? How does Sarah's mom's work connect with Kahlo's and Rivera's work?

8. Why does Sarah decide to break up with David? What eventually convinces her to try again with him?

9. What changes does Sarah's dad make to show that he's serious about dealing with his grief in a healthier way? How does Sarah's life begin to change as a result?

10. Mr. Porter wants Sarah to follow the school's policy of "political neutrality." What is Sarah's counterargument? Do you think it's possible—or desirable—to separate art and politics?

ACKNOWLEDGMENTS

I am always amazed when I see someone speak out about an issue that doesn't affect them personally. So, I would like to first thank Frida Kahlo, Diego Rivera, and U2. In 1954, just days before her death, Frida Kahlo protested the US overthrow of Guatemala's democratically elected president, Jacobo Árbenz. That same year, Diego Rivera painted *Gloriosa Victoria*, a painting that addresses this coup against Guatemala. Even though neither Diego nor Frida were from Guatemala, they used their voices to speak out against the unjust actions of the United States against my native country. I also have to thank U2 for using their music to bring attention to similar atrocities committed in Argentina, Chile, and El Salvador.

Thank you to my husband, Nolan, who played the U2 song "Mothers of the Disappeared" for me, which inspired the idea for Sarah's art project. Nolan has been a great supporter of my writing for over seventeen years, since I first said I want to write a book. He will talk about my books to anyone who will listen.

A big thank-you to my sister, Claudia Armann, who helps make my writing better. I'm so grateful to have a wonderful sister and a great friend all in one. Thank you to my three sons—Omar, Diego, and Ruben—for giving me the most important job title.

Thank you to my parents, Jose and Cory Argueta, who have taught me the most important life lessons—kindness and compassion. Everything I have and everything that I am is from them.

I would like to thank all the wonderful people at Cable Elementary who have shown great support and love. It is a wonderful place to work.

Thank you to my agent, Kathy Green, for answering so many questions and helping me navigate this publishing journey. I will forever be grateful that you loved Millie from *Where I Belong*, which made it possible for us to begin this wonderful working relationship. A big thank-you to Amy Fitzgerald, who has sent me so many emails filled with happy news. Thanks for your dedication to telling this story and helping me figure out how to tell it. I will forever be grateful to Lerner Books for their continual support.

ABOUT THE AUTHOR

Marcia Argueta Mickelson was born in Guatemala and immigrated to the United States as an infant. She is the author of five novels, including the YA novel *Where I Belong*, a Pura Belpré Young Adult Honor book. She lives in Texas with her husband and three sons.